INTERSECT: A LOVE STORY

INTERSECT: A LOVE STORY

Harold Torger Vedeler

iUniverse, Inc.
New York Lincoln Shanghai

Intersect: A Love Story

All Rights Reserved © 2003 by Harold Torger Vedeler

No part of this book may be reproduced or transmitted in any form or by any means, graphic, electronic, or mechanical, including photocopying, recording, taping, or by any information storage retrieval system, without the written permission of the publisher.

iUniverse, Inc.

For information address:
iUniverse, Inc.
2021 Pine Lake Road, Suite 100
Lincoln, NE 68512
www.iuniverse.com

ISBN: 0-595-30435-4

Printed in the United States of America

Prologue

You are a witness.

Don't deny it, and don't turn away. Because I know you. I know what you want, and I know why you're here.

Yes.

You wear the burden of need, heavy on your shoulders. It's eaten at your soul, like it did for the others, for all of those who ride the magtrain to that last little stop at the edge of the map, who beg, borrow or steal a ride along broken roads until at last they arrive here, cold and tired and hungry.

Like you.

Don't deny it and don't turn away; just by coming here you have confessed.

You are a witness.

Yes?

Very well, then. Sit. Relax. Have a cup of something hot and warm your feet by the fire. And remember, too. Always remember, because that is the essence of this thing. If you can, remember what you did, when you rode the wings of heaven, when you danced with the angels. When they touched your soul and made you weep.

Do you?

Remember?

Forgive me. I'm old and prone to digressions. But this is the part of the story you haven't heard, the rest of it, the things you've always thought about, always wondered. I know why things happened when they did.

So be still. Think back.

It's in the papers, of course, and in the old vids. The Game. That's what everyone called it, though it had a real name all its own. People still talk like that today, when they quietly allow themselves to recall. The Game, they say. Where were you during the title match of Lorenzo of Venezuela and Akad of Turkey? York the Canadian and Velasquez of Spain? Remember? The golden girls, the perfect girls? Do you remember how you worshipped them, how people whispered the holy name back and forth to one another on those afternoons when the matches were held?

Yes?

Ah. Good.

But how did it begin? What was the germ, the source, the reason? Think back…concentrate. What was The Game? What did it mean and how did it work? Why did they play and why did we watch? Ask yourself and answer. Look in the mirror and be true to what you see; then you will know. For actually it was simple, in its way, and this should be no surprise. Think about Christianity, Islam, football. Think about Communism and Buddhism and rock-and-roll. Simplicity. Great movements, great ideas, things that can move a million people to action, all of them are built around such simplicity. As much as they may vary they all share this one thing. Here it was no different: The Game was the higher brain, the ecstasy of intellect, of pure knowledge, running through our synapses, bringing to each of us all the potential in our own minds. It was human thought at its highest; an orgasm above the neck instead of below the belt. Not an easy thing to do, no, but possible.

You ask how, by what means.

Here:

Take a computer. Take a person. The computer is the purity and the person is the joy. The machine is the translator and the soul is the message. Mix them, blend them, transmit them. Make them interact, intersect.

Intersect.

Yes!

You know that word. That was its name, back then. The Game. The point of intersection, where the human soul and the pure, mathematical mind of the computer met. Where they joined and built on themselves. Manipulating and ordering pure human thought into a rush of data that we shared at light speed. It was more, too, when they played in pairs, when they dueled with gigabytes and theorems and numbers. The joy and beauty of the human intellect, of all that we were and that we could be, amplified. Amplified, exaggerated, and broadcast into a VR chair that went straight to the soul.

As The Game.

Do the details, the trillions of lines of software, the design of the chips and the physics by which the VR chair connected to our minds, do these matter?

Intersect.

It worked. It connected us to them, to those who played it. We sat in our VR chairs and we watched and lived as they dueled with joy and love. Us, by the billions, watching their souls; those perfect, golden souls.

Intersect. They even fought small wars over it. Over the network lines, over who actually owned the computers that ran it all, over the system, over the trillions and trillions of connections that formed the matrices where they danced. And over the girls, too, who played it.

Girls. Because that was the catch, wasn't it? Only girls. Remember? Because though anyone could sit in a chair and watch, not everyone could play. Playing was a different thing, a special thing. Your brain had to be just right and just right meant female. They found that out right away when a man hooked in and blew out the system; software, hardware, and all. Pow! It was something about his brain, about male brains. Something that crashed it all, every time.

So no men. Ever. Not even primary transsexuals.

Men missed half the joy.

But only half, because they could still watch, and watching made it all worthwhile.

Watching was wonder and joy and beauty and it killed other sports, other hobbies. Why work when you can watch? Why think? Why act?

Why live when an angel can live for you?

So Intersect grew, weathered its scandals, spread its joy over the Earth. It spanned the end of an era and the beginnings of another. Women played first, then girls. Girls were better, beat their mothers hands down. The best became household names, sat with Presidents and Kings, rode through the streets in parades. They were young goddesses, lavished, pampered, envied. They competed for championships and awed the world. Careers were short and players started young—just after puberty was the peak.

It was a girl game.

And the best of the girls was Shannon O'hea.

Chapter 1

That much you can read in the papers and the histories. There's other material too, quite a lot of it, in fact, but for now let's look at Shannon. Not so hard, if you remember, because Shannon was beautiful. Oh, yes; beautiful. And not just your textbook peep mag VR digitally enhanced beautiful, but beyond that. She had a thousand ship face; perfect features, perfect hair that shined like platinum in the light, deep brown eyes set perfectly above a little bump of a nose, a perfect smile. Look at an old photo and your eyes will be drawn to her; look at an old vid and you'll find yourself not paying attention to anything else in it. And take that beauty, that exact, perfect face, and multiply it by ten, twenty, a hundred.

That was Shannon in the matrices. That was the Shannon whose perfect synapses you saw from the VR chair. Is it any wonder that more people knew of her than knew of the Pope?

Shannon O'hea was World Champion.

She was thirteen years old, sitting in a private car on the Transamerican magtrain. Chicago lay ahead, somewhere in the growing gloom of early evening, a city waiting, anticipating, organizing for her. But she was alone right now, sitting in that private car, alone save for her friend Alicia and the stuffed toy panda that lay reclined against one of the padded seats. Once in a while a brief streak of light broke the darkness as another train passed nearby, racing at high speed to somewhere, hurrying as only Americans can.

Shannon O'hea yawned, stretched, pulled back a strand of her perfect hair. Electronic music was playing through the car's sound system and Alicia reached over to adjust the volume. The song was a recent one, singing what each generation thinks is new to them but is not.

I can feel your heartbeat,
its rhythm like my own.
Let me take your hand in mine
like someone's I have known.

The panda belonged to Alicia and now she tugged without thinking at one of its ears. A fan club in England had given it to her, complete with a sewed-in smile and a little medal that had fallen off soon after. She had been new to the game then, alone and afraid, and it had been her companion through the tournament. That was two years ago and now it was less a toy than a keepsake.

You grow up fast as an Intersect girl.

"It's cold," Shannon said.

"Winter soon," Alicia answered, and she yawned.

Shannon turned to her friend and watched her closely. Alicia was pretty but not burdened with beauty, her body young and sexless and unremarkable. But there was a style to her that you saw in the matrices: she loved to dance as she played; she teased and turned and sometimes lost because of it, but it was somehow her and the public loved it.

Now she picked at her nose and rubbed her arm.

"Not as cold as Moscow," Shannon said.

"No."

It grew later. Seven o'clock. Seven-thirty. The music ended and neither of them made any effort to start it up again. A series of lights flashed by outside: the station at Champaign-Urbana.

Behind them the door opened. They swiveled in their chairs and Shannon spoke.

"Mother," she said.

Mother. Mama to a baby, Mommy to a toddler, Mom to an older child. But it was Mother to Shannon; formal, more a title than a name. Mother, a tall, elegant woman, raised in society, in the hurry-hurry of a career in law and then a career in the game. A career now of grooming her daughter, a career that made her distant but devoted, utterly. She did not show love, not Mrs. O'hea, but she felt it and when it was most needed it was there. She stepped forward and spoke.

"Chicago in another hour. We've got your dresses laid out in our car." She paused, looked down at her daughter, extended a hand and cupped it under Shannon's chin. "I think a touch of makeup would be good."

"Yes, Mother." Shannon stood and Alicia did likewise.

Mother smiled. "You're both going to shine this year."

They followed her back through the door and into the next car. Alicia's mother was there, a firm, intent woman built on a heavy frame. She smiled too but it was not so easy for her, not so natural. She stood by a bed and on that bed lay two dresses.

They opaqued the windows and clothes came off and clothes came on. Alicia was handed a brush and gave her short hair its obligatory thirty strokes, settling it back behind her ears. Shannon's hair took longer; it had to be perfect, of course, held in place by a black ribbon, smooth down her back. She sat very still as Mother finished and touched up her face.

"Good…That's good. You know that the Mayor and the Governor are meeting us at the hotel."

"Yes."

"Do you remember their names?"

"The Mayor is Paul Kestel. The Governor is Elizabeth Trigg."

"Good. Hold still now." Gloss on the lips, just a bit. Then a mirror, a moment to consider.

Perfection. Mother stepped back. "Now don't muss it, dear."

"Yes, Mother." Shannon moved back to her car and closed the door behind her. Alicia was already there and the music was on again.

They sat silently. It was a clear night outside and you could see a few stars through the windows. Shannon stared into the dark, blinking now and again, afraid to rest her chin in her hand for fear of tampering with her face. She kept her fingers folded instead, laced one over the other, settled on her lap. Another train flashed by in a brilliant burst of light, then was gone.

Shannon looked into nothing and saw.

Have you ever watched the dark? It holds mysteries, you know. For the fearful these are dangers, terrifying things, but for others the darkness is a place for imagination, for little games played in the mind. What is in it? What does it hold? In the physical world these can be many things; in time only one. Darkness is like the future. It is unknown, uncertain, but infinite in its possibilities. Once in a while Shannon played a game with this, in her head, a secret game that she had never shared. What if I was out there? she thought. What if I was someone out there, some anonymous person in an anonymous place marked only by a passing bit of light?

Someone different?

Not me?

This was what she saw, just for a moment.

Then the nothing of darkness became nothing again. She turned from the window and looked over at Alicia. Her friend.

Always. Because everyone needs a friend, somewhere, sometime. Even the perfect ones, the special ones. Simply to be adored is not enough, for those who adore are seeing not you but the person they want you to be. It is hard to be happy with reality when fantasy is too important, too strong, too perfect.
Intersect would always win.
But there is another kind of love, though, if you are willing to look for it. Not digital, not defined. You see it everywhere but you do not understand it. It is the kind of love that bonds friends and lovers and husbands and wives. It is love up close, love shared by experience, by a common need, a common hope, a common dream, and it is a thing that when you see it will make you stand by and watch with awe. Go back to Moscow now, in the cold of early fall. Go back to St. Basil's and the Kremlin and the calm waters of the Moscow river. Go back to the sleek, silver jets coming in from all around the world, the celebrities and politicians, the tense excitement as each country sent its best, perfect children.
Go back. Shannon was there, and her mother and her Matron. Go back. Alicia too, the strange newcomer who had surprised all the oddsmakers. And the other girls, oh yes: Tanya Kirilova, the little Russian and hometown favorite; Li Yon, adopted daughter of all Nanking; Maria Chavez from Brazil and Monica Chavez from Mexico. Fatima Al-Hakim of Baghdad, Monique Armeneau of Lyons. More too, name after name after name.
Guarded, protected, shuttled here and there by luxury limousine. Competing before the billions.
Yes and fine and very well. They came, they competed, and the world sat in its VR chairs and was hushed with the beauty and the love of the game. Prelims first, week after week, sorting out the best, establishing standings and records and names for the elimination round. Match after match so that every day you could tune in and watch, so you could follow your favorite and dance with her on each matrix, feeling her perfect mind inside your own. And after the matches there was the media, following, analyzing, watching the girls at breakfast, lunch and dinner and sending every moment of the tournament straight into your living room.
But high in the Cosmos Hotel, on the guarded floors, there was more than this. Unsuspected things. Things you did not see. Beginnings in the quiet of an evening, seeds being laid.
This was where it began.

Shannon, lonely, nursing a headache. Imagine her now, a twelve year old girl cut off by distant love from all the other twelve year old girls in the world. Imagine her walking down the carpeted hall, small and beautiful and adored and trapped in her fame. Can you see it? A hand perhaps, rubbing against her temples, her mother away and her Matron sleeping just down the hall. Prelims were over and Shannon was ranked number one; outside her window the sky and the day were gray; inside her room the walls were colorful but bare and the language on the vidset foreign.

Strasvidzya. Dosvedanya.

Go back.

The hall was empty and she paced for a time. There were the other rooms, blank doors with numbers. She reached the elevator and the guard smiled down at her and spoke with an accent.

"Hallo, Miss O'hea."

"Hello."

"I can page an escort. If you would like to go out."

Shannon shook her head. An escort would be Russian and he would escort her in Russia and she had already seen the sites of the city anyway. She turned, moved away. The guard watched her and shifted a bit in his place to get more comfortable.

Other rooms, and behind them other girls. Shannon passed each door without slowing down, lost the gaze of the guard behind a turn in the hall. In these rooms were rivals, competitors. And foreign too, by and large. Li Yon, Maria Chavez, Monique Armeneau. Names, faces that were just familiar, styles of play that Shannon knew better than the back of her hand because at one time or another she had beaten most of them.

Then Shannon reached a door and stopped. Inside her chest she imagined her heart. Beating, more quickly now, harder and harder against her ribs. She could feel it, no longer imaginary, no longer hidden. She extended her little hand and formed a fist, knocked on the door in front of her.

Tap. Tap. A small hand against the wood. Beginnings.

She had not meant to do this, not at first. She was a competitor, ranked number one, and this was her rival. There were unwritten rules here, rules that told her to be afraid and wary, to hide away and plot and vanquish in the matrices. Build walls like a fortress. Hide yourself behind them because everyone out there wants inside, wants to pick you apart. Move away now and forget you ever did this.

But Shannon did not move and after a moment the door opened.

Alicia watched her for a few seconds.

"Hi," Shannon said.

"Hi." The voice was guarded and the young face impassive.

"You doing anything?"

Alicia paused. She was wearing a hotel robe that was just a bit big for her and now she tightened the belt.

"Was gonna watch some vid," she said.

Shannon nodded. The fingers on her right hand fidgeted. "Oh."

Alicia looked down, then up again. "You want to watch?"

"Okay."

Shannon stepped inside.

They had these things in common: American English. Elementary school and the anticipation of Junior High. Pizza, hamburgers, root beer and cola. I pledge allegiance to the flag...Presidents on their money and Thanksgiving turkey in November.

All these things and more, in that little room.

"You listen to the New Boyz?"

"Oh, yeah. They're good. You like them too?"

"I got their latest album. It's the best."

"Look at the case. I got them to sign mine when I met them last year."

"Wow."

Jingle bells. Easter bunny. Fourth of July.

"We always open half our presents on Christmas Eve."

"Why?"

"My dad says that was really Jesus' birthday, so we should."

"We never do. Just church."

"They got funny looking churches around here, don't you think?"

"Yeah. Kinda."

Inside jokes and inside stories and ways of looking at the strange, foreign vid together that neither had alone. Look at that! What did he say? No, don't touch the translator! Let me guess! Let me guess! Ways of talking, familiar slang. Cool. Scoping on boys. Zoning. American things because they were American girls. Laughing, joking finally, a little island of similarities in a sea of differences.

Many things. Can you remember all you said to your first friend?

All around them Moscow went on, settling into sleep that evening in its uniquely Russian way, unaware, uncaring, awaiting the matches of tomorrow.

And Moscow was the first to see as they sat at dinner together the next day and talked quietly among themselves.

Well, then, look at this, someone said.

Surprised? They're both American.

I'm not sure Alicia's Matron approves. Look how she's scoping on them.

Never mind. Tomorrow starts the first round. Shannon pairs off with that Australian.

She's gonna cream 'er.

I know.

I know.

It went on. Eliminations. Every day you would rise, watch the board or the vid, see how you stood. Who's next? How tough are they? Leotard and tights and warm-ups, down to the lobby, past the powerful lights of the cameras, into the limo and off to Moscow University. Tension in you like a knot, pulling tighter as you step into your chamber, as you wait for them to call your name. You try not to think about it, about what the sportscasters said, about how the whole country is betting on you, how you dare not let them down.

Adrenaline burning your veins. You have to pee suddenly. You alert the officials and go but it does not help. And through the wait, the tightness in your gut, you realize that you love it all, every minute, every waiting second.

"O'hea, Van Hoost."

The words come as a blessing. You rise, slip into the special VR chair designed for the game, signal that you are ready, hook into the abstract reality of the matrices. You are connected now, a piece of every home, facing billions of minds. It is a rush, a high. You are goddess, queen mother, queen bee. You relax now, watch for your opponent, organize your thoughts and your strategy. You are pure potential, refined, honed.

Victorious. Triumphant in joy. You can feel them, all the billions out there, calling to you in thanks, in gratitude, in love. You emerge and you smile for the cameras and you are one round closer to the prize. Questions from the reporters now: Brilliant! Are you ready for the next match? How did you counter her there? And there?

Later, you think back.

How you answered, you smiled, you waved. America's girl. You boarded your limousine and you let them drive you back to the hotel, where you went upstairs and lay down, tired. Mother came in and rubbed your back and later got you dressed for dinner. You ate and watched the cameras watching you, smiled a perfect smile for them, and then you went back up to your room where you went to bed. And as the lights went out and you closed your eyes, you knew that tomorrow would be just the same.

Yes. Remember. How it went, how it felt as we watched. Match after match, day after day. Weeding out the elite. Fatima Al-Hakim, shy beneath her white hijab, upset Li Yon, then fell to Tanya Kirilova. Two Asian countries expelled one another's diplomats after a close match, restored them three days later after the United Nations intervened. Alicia stunned the world over Monica Chavez. Shannon powered her way past Junghare. And as the two Americans continued to advance, rumors built over the time they spent together.

What is it with them? What do they talk about? How can they possibly be friends?

Intersect girls are never friends. The stakes are too high.

Then the survivors were down to eight and the questions gathered into one.

What if they meet in the finals?

Alicia sat in Shannon's room. She was staring out the window at the old space monument, streaking upward just across the street. Shannon was lying on the bed. The vid was on but neither paid it much attention.

"Shannon?" Alicia asked.

"Yeah?"

"How long have you been playing?"

Shannon thought for a moment. "About five years."

Alicia went back to looking outside. "You ever have any other friends?" she asked.

"Other friends?"

"In the game."

"No." Shannon shook her head.

"Me neither. I wonder why?"

Shannon sat up, licked at dry lips. Her voice was suddenly even, cold, adult. "This game bares your soul," she said. "You win by tearing down the best thing your opponent ever made. I don't think that makes for lasting friendships."

Alicia nodded but did not look back. She knew this already but admitting it was more than she dared. Shannon leaned forward, rested her chin in her hands, looked over at Alicia. Alicia spoke slowly and softly.

"What if we have to play?"

"Then we play," Shannon answered.

Alicia's voice trembled slightly. "That's it?"

Shannon looked down at her feet. Her voice softened a bit but it was still firm. "No. Whatever happens, I'm going to win."

Just like that. It was not bragging, Alicia knew. She had seen Shannon play and she knew how good she was. But the words had hit a point of envy in her and she answered without thinking.

"How can you be sure?"

"Because that's what I came here to do."

"And if you don't?"

Shannon said nothing but turned away. Alicia stood in her place for a few minutes and then walked to the door. Silently she opened it, knowing that Shannon was watching her, that words now would mean nothing. She closed the door behind her and walked back to her room, where she lay down on her own bed and began to cry.

The next day both of them won their matches and advanced to the quarterfinals.

The rest is easy to see. It's in the books, in the histories. They were together, but they were apart. Friends but with something hinging on it, each watching the other and perhaps wondering. They were the story of the games, followed through the city and across Red Square to the giant GUM department store. What will they buy, these two little American girls? Look at how Alicia looks at that dress in the window! Will Shannon really wear those amber earrings?

Oh, I hope so.

Yes, I hope so.

They spoke? What did they say? A challenge, maybe? A gauntlet, thrown down? Only four left, you know. Tomorrow we'll know, won't we?

Shannon was the youngest World Champion ever at Sydney. It wasn't a fluke, either; look at the vids from Cairo last year.

But Alicia is unorthodox. Shannon isn't used to that.

What do you say, Shannon?

What do you say?

Ah. Go back and watch the vids. Look how Shannon turns away, shaking her head slightly, that faint smile on her face. What was she thinking then? Was she that certain?

Was she surprised when Tanya Kirilova beat Alicia the next day to move into the title match with her?

No one knows. But the games went on. Alicia faced off with Monique Armeneau and won in a thriller that left the world weeping with joy. Reporters scrambled to talk with her, to hear what her strategy had been, to photograph her as she smiled and waved. And then the excitement faded, and the cameras turned away, and the eyes and VR chairs of billions were focused on the title match.

Shannon and Tanya. Tanya had been fourth last year in Cairo and she had only gotten better. She entered the game with a flourish, with power and grace and awesome ability. She was good, even brilliant.

But it was never a match. Shannon moved through the matrices like no one ever had before. Her play, her control, her steps, all were perfect. She disassembled Tanya, dissected her at a rate of a trillion bytes a second. She extended her tendrils into every corner of the network, drew theorems of pure mathematical love that had never before been conceived. She wove a beauty that was ideal and yet seemed so accessible, just there, right in front of you as you sat in your VR chair. And the people of the world wept and cheered and wondered how mankind had ever done without the wonderful game and the golden girls who played it.

Shannon, first place. World champion. Alicia, third. Bronze medal. Bring them home! the people cried. Let us salute them! Bring them home to parades and a meeting with the President and offers of millions to endorse a doll or a cake!

Sweethearts. Too young to have disappointed us.

Alicia should have had the silver. She slips, tries for the artistic stuff. Ought to stick to fundamentals.

Pity about that Indonesian girl.

Next year. Next year it'll be one—two—three. That little Ellen Rodriguez is up and coming.

And Shannon is at her peak.

Yet did we see more? Did we look?

No. We didn't care, you see. We were entranced by what we lived in our VR chairs and we didn't notice as the first seeds were planted, seeds that would lay the entire world low.

Last year Moscow.

This year Chicago.

The magtrain sped onward into the silent night.

Chapter 2

▼

They call it the windy city, and like Moscow the year before, people came. They filled hotels and hostels, just to be there. It was America's turn now, to show the world, for the American team was strong this year, stronger than ever before.

The crowds turned out for their heroines. They pressed against the guardrails of the magtrain station, hoping and praying for just a look, even just a glimpse, of the radiantly beautiful Shannon O'hea and Alicia the dancer.

A glimpse, a wave, a smile or a nod.

Look! Lights down the track!

That's only the eight o'clock from Minneapolis.

Large and small the people came, gathering, clustering, talking in hushed tones. Mothers and fathers brought their little girls to show what would make them proud, repeated the word over and over to the little ears.

Intersect.

Intersect.

Sportscasters brought predictions and questions. They sat for long hours on the vids, discussing, analyzing. Shannon will repeat, most of them said. Almost no doubt about it. Let's show our viewers a cut from last year's championship match.

Look at that move! A trillion bytes, up, down! Look at that construct!

Let's see how she defended it!

Boys came too, to the terminal at Chicago. All kinds of boys: big and little, black and white and brown. Boys from rich families and poor families and broken families. They were as different as any group of American boys can be, but those who came all shared one thing: They had seen Shannon or Alicia, had sat in their VR chairs and bathed in perfect, machine-pure love. They had put posters of Shannon or Alicia on their bedroom walls, flanked by music stars and football players, but bigger, higher. And each boy, awash in pubescent hormones and imprinted by the game, had the notion that maybe he could get Shannon O'hea or Alicia the dancer to love him too.

This is all in the news; in the interviews with the average man, the average woman, the average boy. You know this because hero worship is among the oldest of human institutions. But if you look at the vids of the arrival of the magtrain from St. Louis, just there, near the front, you will see someone who was never interviewed, who was never seen or noticed.

His name was Georgie Collins, and he was fifteen, and he was like all the others.

He was in love with Shannon O'hea.

He had waited at the station for six hours for her to come. He had her pictures on his bedroom wall. He wrote her love letters that opened his soul and that were never answered. Because of her he had studied Intersect and knew all the rules, all the terms.

Now he fought to keep a grip on the rail by the gate, pushing against a man on the one side and a woman on the other, so he could see his goddess when she emerged.

He waited, held his breath against the noise as the magtrain slid to a stop. People stepped from the train; first the average passengers, then those who were merely first class. Then security; strong men who scanned the crowd with eyes and sensors, turned back to the door, opened it again.

And then she emerged. Georgie memorized her, scarcely saw the thin girl beside her. She wore a simple dress, his Shannon, with a bit of fashionable flicker at the neck. Someone stepped on his foot; it was a tall girl, her eyes glazed with envy and love and hate. Perhaps she too had seen Shannon's final move in Moscow; perhaps she too could feel what Georgie felt, right now.

Oh, to be this close!

The crowd roared, drowning out his scream. He saw Shannon smile, wave. And Georgie could not help but think that she was waving right at him, to him.

The security men pushed forward, assisted by the police. The crowd pulsed against their arms and Georgie pulsed with them, crying and shouting her name.

"Shannon! Shannon!"

She reached the car then, paused, turned. Someone pressed against him, cursing. It was a father, a big man, his little girl on his shoulders. He shoved Georgie again.

"Hey!" Georgie cried.

"Move it, asshole!" the man barked back.

There was a rail just behind. Georgie saw it, turned, climbed atop it, braced himself with one hand against the wall. He saw as Shannon waved again, tried to wave back as she disappeared into the car.

"Shannon!" he cried, but the car was gone. He climbed back down, let the flow of the crowd take him out of the terminal. There was an ecstasy in him that was almost that of the game itself; he had seen her, his Shannon, and she had waved to him. And then, rising inside him, up and up from his heart to his head, the impossible feeling came.

Maybe, just maybe, she could be his.

He got home late and dinner was cold. His mother was in the den, watching something on the vid. He went to the refrigerator and reached inside for a carton of milk.

"You're late," Mom called out.

Georgie didn't answer and she said nothing more. He found his dinner in the microwave, heated it for thirty seconds and took it out. As he was finishing a commercial came on the vid and Mom stepped into the kitchen. She scowled down at him.

"You mind telling me where you were all day?"

"School. Then I went to the mall."

"Don't lie to me. I called the school and they said you hadn't come in. I was about ready to call the police."

"Did you call the mall too?" he sneered.

She reared up. "Don't take that tone with me! I'll talk to your father!"

She would, too. So he said, "I had stuff to do."

"What stuff?"

He was getting red and hot and he didn't like it much. "Just stuff! Leave me alone!" He was on his feet now and she had settled into her scowl, her hands on her hips and her body stiff.

"I *will* tell your father," she warned again.

"Tell him what? He cut school all the time and so did you! You told me yourself!"

"Georgie—"

But Georgie had turned away and was stalking to his room. They never understood him. Not ever. It wasn't fair but it was true. They didn't get it that he was different than they were, that he needed room because he had dreams that were bigger than this house, this neighborhood, this city. He reached his room and closed the door, switched on the light, went to his bed and lay down.

From the big poster on the facing wall, Shannon O'hea stared down at him.

There was a mystery to her smile that you could get lost in. It was in her eyes too, the way the light played off her face. Like she was talking to him, just him, like the way she had waved this evening, just a few hours ago, at the magtrain station. Georgie closed his eyes and wondered for a moment where she was, right now. He imagined her at the window of her hotel, staring at the city lights.

She's looking, he thought, looking out over the city for someone special, someone to ease her loneliness. Because it must get lonely up there, in those fancy hotels with people who don't really love you, who only hang on to you because you're famous and rich. I wouldn't be like that. I would love you, Shannon, because you make me happy. And you would love me because my love would be sincere, honest. Right from the heart. And we could get away and you could do Intersect for me, just for me, and I would guard you, faithfully, from all those other people who just want to use you.

Shannon, oh my Shannon...

Georgie turned in his unkempt bed and pressed his face against his pillow. There was a warm feeling in his belly, a rush that tickled his shoulders and made him shiver. Outside his door he could hear his mother and father talking, and he knew that soon enough his father would come in here and the yelling would begin.

But for now it was him, alone with his Shannon in the safety of his room. And that was enough.

He smiled.

You doubt, I think. You can believe in a Shannon O'hea but not a Georgie Collins. Consider this, then: Georgie was not unique. Not to his time, not to his place, not to his culture. The game did not make him and neither did Shannon O'hea. There were Georgies alive before either; they screamed out for the Beatles, for Elvis, for Jesus Christ and the Ayatollah. They thronged at the funeral of Nasser and they formed lines at the tomb of Lenin for seventy years. There is a Georgie in each of us, hidden sometimes, but there. It lies in our hopes, our dreams. It builds mankind up, keeps us moving forward a step at a time, gives us an idealism that no other creature has.

And it can destroy us, too, if we aren't careful.

Georgie got up the next day and went to school. His mother went with him to be sure he got there, driving him herself and scowling as she did because she was missing one of her soaps and the vidrecorder was an old model that could only record one show at a time.

"There," she said as they stopped. "Come straight home, understand?"

"Yeah."

The morning passed with English and math and social studies. Georgie was far from brilliant but far from stupid and like most boys his age had only a limited attention span. Twice the teacher caught him daydreaming.

Where did his Shannon go to school?

Maybe she didn't have to. Maybe she was just so smart they had graduated her and all she had to do was dance in the matrices.

"Mr. Collins?"

He looked up. "Huh?"

"How many Justices sit on the Supreme Court?"

He glanced quickly over the book in front of him. Nothing. "Six," he guessed finally.

"Did you read the assignment from yesterday?"

He lied. "Yeah."

"It was in there. Don't you remember it? How many Justices, Mr. Collins?"

"Four."

"Never mind, Mr. Collins. Anyone else?"

Lunch came and he sat with Jim and Adam and they toyed with the food on the trays in front of them. Jim and Adam followed Intersect too and the three of them talked in hushed tones.

"You gonna watch the prelims?"

"Oh yeah. Shannon's on at eight tomorrow."

"You got a schedule already?"

"My dad. Went by the station and picked one up."

"Cool."

Adam was lucky. His father was a big fan and he always had first line information. Georgie drank from his milk carton and as he finished he crushed it in a display of machismo.

"I saw them yesterday," he bragged.

"Who?"

"Shannon. And Alicia."

"You lying shit," Adam said, suddenly upstaged.

"Where, dude?" Jim asked.

"Magtrain station."

"That's where you were all day?"
Georgie nodded.
"Magnum cool," Jim said.
They ate some more. Across the way a cluster of girls gathered, talking and giggling. Jim watched them closely. Adam spoke softly to Georgie.
"I know where they're staying."
"Huh?"
"Shannon, dude. The Intersect girls. My dad got the dirt from a guy he knows."
"Wow."
"We could scope it. After school?"
Georgie nodded. "Yeah. Cool."

They took the L south, walked to the lakefront. It was chilly out, and the wind blew in from off the lake. Jim hunched his shoulders under his thin jacket.
"I'm cold," he said.
"Wimp," teased Adam.
Georgie was silent. He felt all warm again, like he had at the station. He looked up at the glass face of one of the towering skyscrapers, wondered if someone could see them down here, if they looked. Maybe with binoculars, or if he did something to attract attention. A flare gun, maybe?
Adam led them south, past the Field Museum and Soldier Field. Cars went by, sometimes alone and sometimes in groups. A few had tinted windows that made them appear almost sinister. The wind picked up a bit and Jim shivered.
"Here we are," Adam said finally. "Claremont Downtown."
They stared for several minutes. The Claremont Downtown consisted of two towers, two wings. These formed a certain symmetry to the hotel's facade, an elegance to the architecture. As the boys watched a limousine pulled up to the front and three people emerged.
"They've got the entire north tower set aside for the Intersect girls," Adam said.
"Let's see if we can get inside," Jim said.
Adam looked at Georgie. "Want to?"
Georgie looked at his friends. Suddenly he was afraid. Not that they would get caught but that they wouldn't. What if they got inside, up to the secret floors where the athletes stayed? What if they found Shannon's room and knocked and she let them in?

His friends were suddenly rivals. With three to chose from, would she pick him?

He shook his head. "Nah. My dad busts me again…"

"Wimp," Adam said.

"Too many cops," Georgie added, and to his relief Jim nodded.

They walked back to the L station and as they did each of them would sometimes turn and look back at the hotel. Georgie smiled slightly; the warm feeling was still there.

Chapter 3

She swam in the seas of heaven, an abstraction among the perfect ideas of numbers and algorithms and constructs. Far away, across theorems that she saw as lines drawn and redrawn with blessed symmetry, there was another like her.

Like but not like. She raised up and redrew what she was, even as the other, not so distant now, erased what she had been.

The battle began in earnest.

Theorem, construct. Ideas that took on form in perfect mathematics, shifting, shaping. Herself in motion, grace, beauty, pure emotion of intellect. Pure joy in the dance that was a trillion bytes processing, crossing, competing.

For the other, that was in life Maria Chavez, did the same.

Build and rise and fall in grace. Quantify the surge of love. Break it down, analyze it, and scatter it to the matrix. Maneuver in pirouettes of processing lines, across and down. Quiet now, let her come. There is caution in her beauty but you expect that you expect that almost…almost…now!

And the construct split, divided. Irrational numbers growing and overloading and that sudden rush to protect yourself against the very thing you have just used on her. Rationalize, hold, spin…

Bow, my dear.

Bow because they love you too.

The city had chosen the Museum of Science and Industry and had sealed off an entire floor for the competition. It was all they needed and it was not difficult to restrict access. When the championship was over part of it was to become a permanent exhibit, courtesy of an act of Congress. Nearby, the University of Chicago provided vital support.

One by one they tested the girls. Identity first, through DNA and neural patterning. Compatibility to the system, which was an hour spent hovering in the Nirvana of computer unbeing. When it was over the Matrons brought food and the mothers sat with their daughters and some of them took tours through the museum and over to the University to see where long ago nuclear fire had first been controlled.

Prelims began then. Random matchings. Feeling the waters, testing the strategies.

Below, in the museum's central hall, reporters gathered, standing, sitting, writing or whispering notes into recorders.

We have over a hundred young women here. Each one wants to be World Champion. Each one wants to take the glory home. Watch these pairings. A rematch here, from Moscow. Will Li Yon avenge herself against the Iraqi?

Look! On the balcony! Get the camera up!

Shannon O'hea and Tanya Kirilova!

Did you see how Shannon handled Maria Chavez?

That's good…wave now…fine, fine. Got it. Put that out on tonight's vid. I sense a rating boost.

How much did this coverage cost the network?

Never mind.

The girls vanished back into the converted galleries and the reporters went back to their whispering. And the day passed and the sun set and the city slept, anticipating.

Anticipating. Kadeja Manzo. Kadeja's play was subtle. She crept up on you, carefully distracting with flourishes while from behind a tendril of impossibility rose, disassembling, shattering. And then you were no more and you didn't even know why.

But she could be beaten if you knew this.

And Shannon did. Shannon knew all about her because Shannon had taken her out of the early rounds in Moscow. She studied that match now, the records, watched herself and Kadeja parry with gigabytes, froze and replayed this sequence and that, wondered if a year had taught Kadeja anything new.

Probably. Best to be careful.

It was quiet in the hotel room, at the large desk by the bed where Shannon sat. She watched the match again, set the little computer aside. Another review tonight and she would be ready.

Or not tonight. Tonight was the reception at the opera house. Maybe she ought to head back early, claim fatigue. *I'm only a little girl, after all.*

She rose, stepped to the mirror, touched at her hair, smiled ruefully. And she knew the lie and wondered when they would come to know it too. *I'm not a little girl, not anymore. Maybe I never was; when was the last time I felt that way?*

Long ago. Before Intersect. Before that day when they had taken all the little girls in her class and had sat each of them in a VR chair and that funny looking man had watched the computer next to her and had given her instructions.

All right, Shannon. Do you see that line? Can you cut it in half? Concentrate. Put yourself between it. Good…Good. Now, more lines. Can you?

This is fun.

Excellent, Shannon. Excellent. Go stand with your friends now.

Can I try it again?

She remembered the smile on his face but hadn't understood it. *Oh, yes, Shannon. Soon.*

Soon. Training, coaches. A new school that everyone said was better. And the looks on the old faces; Michelle, Rose, Lisa. New looks from her friends who weren't in the new school, and who after a while weren't her friends anymore.

Long ago. In the system, in the matrices. Hours a day. Coaches, Matrons, an agent. *Practice, Shannon, there isn't much time. You'll get old, soon enough, and there'll be plenty of time then. Keep at it.*

Weeks, months. Better and better and better. A tournament; first place. Another. She remembered first seeing her own face on the vid: Southwest Regional Champion.

Work, Shannon. Work. Never settle for less than perfection.

Never. One day she went back to her old school, and in front of the entire class she stood. Try Intersect, girls, she said. Be like me. I have it all. And she had found Michelle and Rose and Lisa and they had talked, but it was not the same.

There was no old life anymore.

But there was the new. Mr. This and Mrs. That, telling her what she should do, how she should act and sit and behave. Telling her again and again as one year became two how good she was, how wonderful. And the trophies then, the medals. Now.

Shannon looked over at the vid, off now, sitting silently. She stared at it for a moment and smiled.

Shannon O'hea, America's girl.
Shannon, why do you use Kleen-Smile?
You ask me, John, she's the best ever. You ever see a match like that?
Hello, Madame President. Hello, Shannon. We're all so proud of you.
Of you.
Of you.
Of me.

Later, Mother returned. Shannon was at the computer again, reviewing, testing, thinking. She turned at the sound of the door.

"Mother."

Mother nodded. Shannon returned to her work. There was a way to stack irrational numbers that aligned an irrational joy with a gentle sound that went straight through the matrices and broke through two classical defenses. But you had to do it right, just right, or it all fell apart.

York had done it once. Why not me?

No reason. You certainly can.

But not right away. Save this one for Tanya in the eliminations.

Shannon smiled to herself.

She finished, satisfied, and turned. Mother was watching the vid with the earphones on. She saw Shannon turn and switched the thing off.

"We should get ready," she said, and Shannon nodded.

There was a certain pleasure in preparation. Picking just how to look, anticipating mood and feeling. Showing everyone just what you wanted to show them. Mother knew this, understood that beauty is a two part thing, that it lies in the viewer and the viewed, that it is active and that you must be able to read the person who sees you.

Like Mother could, even off the vid. She knew how to express mood and how to change it through the day, how to fit it to the powerful or how to make you seem like anybody's girl just next door.

I want to be innocent, you might say. I want to intimidate. And you were and you did.

Shannon bathed, relaxed for a few minutes in perfumed water, toweled herself dry and washed her hair in the large sink. She sat still in her robe as Mother combed back the strands and worked in a bit of curl at the ends. She dressed carefully and stood for inspection, relaxed her face for makeup, for small earrings, for a little necklace and bracelet that were worth more than the lifetime earnings of most of the world. She carried no purse; everything she might need was with Mother and nothing should be allowed to disturb what was perfect symmetry.

She faced the mirror again, smiled, turned. She looked over at her mother.

"We'll need to be back early," she said. "I want to review for my match tomorrow."

"Of course." Mother stepped forward, stared at her for a moment.

"To think…" she began.

Shannon cocked her head, raised a perfect eyebrow. With one finger she touched at the diamonds on her bracelet.

Mother smiled. Her face had shifted a bit, just on the edge of wistful. And she spoke softly.

"This is your year, Shannon. This is your time. I can feel it."

"What do you mean, Mother?"

A smile, then. A touch on her young shoulder. A whisper.

"Listen, Shannon. Not everyone gets what they want in life. But you have. Someday you'll look back on this tournament and you'll know that it was the best time of your life. Cherish it."

They moved together to the door.

Mozart; The Marriage of Figaro. Less a performance for Chicago than for the world, to show that America, land of fads, of speed and greed, of Hollywood and Las Vegas, that America could be civilized if it wanted to be, that it had culture and art and appreciation. Bring your children, the Americans said, your finest, and we will show them these things.

They brought Shannon and the others in small groups, led them past security men and into the theater's large atrium. There was a display of modern art there, sculpture and paintings, and a table with punch and refreshments. Waiters in tuxedos, moving with trays.

The mayor. Breaking from a group, taking her hand gently.

"Miss O'hea! A pleasure! May I introduce you to Councilwoman Espinoza?"

A smile, just right. "Of course. A pleasure, Madame. A pleasure."

"All mine, Miss O'hea. I wanted to thank you personally for gracing our fine city."

"You've all been very kind. The gratitude is mine."

The woman smiled just as Shannon knew she would.

The reception passed; a glass of punch, a bit of cake, eaten with delicate fingers. Smiles here and there, graceful movement, bits of conversation and names remembered and that look on people's faces when they were.

Congressman. Director. Corporate president. And there was no effort to it, no energy.

She was Shannon O'hea and they came to her.

The lights dimmed, came on again. Mother had the tickets and Shannon went with her up to the balcony.

And Figaro began his measurements as he sang.

The opera went on, scene and song and orchestra. Shannon sat and Shannon watched and she knew as she did that she was a part of it too, a part of the performance, that the eyes of others were on her as much as they were on the stage, watching, thinking, expecting.

Expecting what?

This. Poise, perfection.

She did not move save to blink. Her foot itched through a duet, through an aria, but she was stone against it. Maybe she could slip off her shoe, rub the spot with her other toe, but then her knee would move and one of the watchers would take notice and it would have to mean something. No, this was easier, better. She was Shannon O'hea and that by itself meant everything.

Then the second act ended and the lights came on for intermission. She rose with the others. A man approached as she did, shook her hand, explained how pleased he was to meet her, how he loved the game and might she be so kind as to autograph his program?

Of course. Here you are.

Thank you. Thank you.

She followed Mother out. The atrium was crowded and there was a fresh bowl of punch by the paintings. Shannon moved that way, smiling, stepping, nodding as people greeted her. The waiter spooned a glass for her, watched her closely as she took it. She stepped away.

And then another man was there.

"Miss O'hea? Miss Shannon O'hea? A pleasure."

He was heavy and well dressed and there was a woman beside him, in a rich gown and pearls and high heels, and this woman beamed as the man spoke again.

"Randolph Dixon. Dixon Transportation. This is my wife, Helen."

Shannon took the outstretched hand. "Nice to meet you."

They beamed and smiled, suddenly out of things to say. Then Dixon turned and extended his hand behind him.

"Oh, and our daughter, Elena."

Elena.

Shannon looked. She saw but did not see.

She was older but still young, Elena. Perhaps sixteen, perhaps a bit more. Dark hair, curled. Two earrings in each pierced ear. A brown skirt and a black sweater and a small face that said nothing.

Shannon extended her hand with her practiced smile.

"Hello, Elena."

A pause. "Hi."

"We're really, *very* big fans, Shannon," Mr. Dixon said. "We were so proud after Moscow."

"Thank you."

"Can I go now?" asked Elena.

Her mother shot her a glare, twitched in discomfort. "All right, then," she answered, and then she looked over at her husband with a sigh. He reddened, just a bit.

And Shannon stared as the girl moved away.

You don't know Elena, but you should.

"I'm sorry," Mr. Dixon said. "She can be difficult."

"That's all right."

And then the Mayor again, with two more councilmen. More hands on hers and more smiles and more greetings and it's a pleasure thank you Shannon thank you Shannon because of you we're proud to be Americans. Finally a break and an empty punch cup and moving away and back to the bowl. Shannon stood in place and sipped from her new cup until she felt the eyes of the waiter on her again. She stepped away to the paintings.

The crowd was thinner here, only one or two among the stands, walking around one of the sculptures. Shannon sighed, closed her eyes for a few seconds. It was getting late and perhaps she should get Mother and head back to the hotel. She passed one canvas, turned to look at another, and saw.

Elena.

Watching her. Closely, intent, but silent. Shannon looked down without knowing why.

Look and listen. You remember the game, and the billions who followed it, who watched, who wept with joy. You remember the crowds and the vids and the sportscasters. The money, the adulation, the worship. But there was more in the world than these, more than what you saw.

You believe that everyone loved Intersect?

Nothing is loved by everyone, my friend. Nothing. There are always exceptions, always a few who go a different way. We deny them, and when denial fails we condemn them and punish them, or we see in them that spark that we then envy, and we emulate them and pretend we understand them. Watch them, these ones. Watch as these ones are burned as witches and watch as they are hailed as saints. Look at them because they affect you, regardless. Remember them. Sometimes you only know them much, much later, when your life has turned on its head and you start to wonder why. Sometimes.

Elena?

Perhaps.

Shannon?

Maybe.

Elena. One step, two, three and four. To Shannon. Narrow eyes, looking, as Shannon's gaze rose. What did Elena want? An autograph, a photo?

A word or two?

She stopped. Nothing. Shannon spoke.

"Hello."

Elena's eyes moved, just caught her. A dark voice with an edge to it.

"Hi."

Shannon looked at the painting beside her. It was dark, abstract, the canvas invisible behind heavy layers of paint. Something in the center almost moving in deep yellows and a bit of gold, and something more. Shannon spoke again to make conversation.

"What is it?"

Elena answered after a pause. "This?" She shrugged. "I don't know." But Elena wasn't watching the painting. After a moment Shannon found her stare uncomfortable.

She spoke to break the pause. "It's almost like it moves."

"Maybe."

Shannon turned her gaze on the girl.

"What is it?" she asked again.

This time Elena answered slowly.

"You."

Silence amidst the noise of surrounding conversation.

"Me?"

"I had to know," Elena said then. Shannon watched her face. Envy brought expressions, usually rage and anger thinly veiled, just ready to break out. It was better to leave when you saw them because anything you might say would only make it worse.

Elena again. "I had to know."

Expressions to fear. Expressions you could not help but know.

But these were not visible, now, on Elena. No envy, no anger. Something different, so Shannon answered with a question.

"Know what?"

Elena's face, calm, eyes no longer narrow. The voice, still different, questioning by its tone. "If you were what I thought you would be. What they said you would be."

"And what was that?"

Elena chuckled. "An Intersect girl."

Shannon looked into nothing and saw.

Fear, unease maybe. Different, honest. Shannon spoke and her voice was suddenly soft.

"Only?"

"That's the only part you show."

Shannon looked. Only. Elena watched her. Perhaps sixteen, perhaps a bit more. Dark hair, curled. Two earrings in each pierced ear. A brown skirt and a black sweater and a small face that said nothing.

Or that said more.

I am Elena. I am a person. Flesh and blood and mind. I have a father and a mother and I have friends and interests and things I do. Look into me and you will see them. Come to know me and you will come to know them, for they are what I am and they are what make me complete.

What are you, Shannon O'hea? What will I see if I look into you?

Elena watched her.

Shannon looked away.

The lights above dimmed and came on again.

Chapter 4

▼

Home was a box in a neighborhood filled with boxes. Simple lawns, back yards filled with old junk that was not quite ready for the landfill or the recycling center but was not quite worth keeping either. Home was anonymous, blended in between the Joneses and the Riveras. It was nothing special and you could live your whole life there and never mean anything.

Like Mom had, and Dad, and Mr. and Mrs. Jones and Mr. and Mrs. Rivera. Get up, go to work, come home, watch the vid. Up, work, home, vid. Up, work, home, vid. Over and over, counting for nothing and meaning nothing.

Sound familiar? Are you one of them? Or do you have dreams?

Georgie did.

It is entirely possible that had there never been Intersect or Shannon O'hea that Georgie would have dreamed anyway. Perhaps in him there was an author, or a painter, or a scholar or a diplomat. Perhaps what drove him towards Shannon would have driven him anyway, would have brought him against the odds and out of the box where dreams are an enemy to be crushed in favor of conformity.

Perhaps.

There is no telling, of course. What might have been might have been and speculation there becomes quickly pointless. What we do know is this: Georgie did dream. It made him an average student but an exceptional boy regardless. It brought him reprimands from his teachers and scoldings at home, but it drove him too and gave him a window out of the cocoon of mediocrity.

A box, a pitched roof, three windows along a street in north Chicago. Georgie turned at the open gate, walked up to the door and stepped inside. It seemed dim even though the lights were on, the floor touched with traces of dirt and a thin layer of dust on the table by the kitchen. In the living room he could hear the vid and he knew that Mom was in the VR chair with one of her soaps.

He took his knapsack back to his room, set it on the bed. There was homework but that could wait. He turned on the computer that sat on his desk and accessed the internet, paged through the news.

Massacre in Rwanda.

Yemeni Ambassador to Israel Recovering From Wounds Received in Assassination Attempt.

Status of White Males as Minority Group Reaffirmed in Supreme Court Decision.

Georgie passed these by, found the main menu and accessed sports. What he wanted was at the very front.

Intersect Match Results.

Prelims, so they didn't matter much. Just to establish rankings and give the world a taste of what was to come, just to let each nation see its girls in the championships, even if they stood no chance. There were more matches this year than last, more competitors, more results. Names and nations and statistics.

Thompson (AUS.) over Yamada (JAP.). Hanik (CZE.) over Feng-hsi (CHI.). Kirilova (RUS.) over Qafisheh (EGT.).

Next page. Next.

Rodriguez (USA) over Gonzalez (HON.).

Next. Next.

There.

O'hea (USA) over Manzo (PHL.).

Georgie sighed and sat back. Of course Shannon had been a heavy favorite, but upsets were real and too many in the prelims got you a bad place on the final docket. He looked over at her stats so far: three wins, no losses. At this point that meant little and there were no rankings yet, but it was still worth following.

Especially since it was here, in this city. Not far away in Moscow or Cairo or cities he couldn't even find in the atlas. He shivered a bit at the thought, at the knowledge of her proximity. Only a few miles south of here, along the lake. He thought about the hotel, the glass facade reaching skyward. I could go there, he said to himself. Just me. Get inside when the security man isn't looking, go up to her room, knock on the door. And she'd open it and I'd say just the right thing and she'd let me in.

Georgie closed his eyes now, relaxed. What would his Shannon say? How would he answer?

Hello, I'm Shannon, and I'm so alone.

Not now, Shannon. Not ever again.

Never?

And Georgie shook his head. It seemed silly but he couldn't banish the thought. How could she be alone when the whole world was watching her? He knew he wasn't the only one, that other boys by the millions loved her too, that they saw her when she played, that when her face came on the vid for a commercial or in a magazine for an ad that they were watching. Seeing her, wanting her.

Like he did.

Shannon O'hea was probably the least alone person in the world.

But the feeling stayed in him; contradictory, impossible. She had everything but the more Georgie thought about it the more he wondered. What does that mean? Can having everything leave you with nothing? Did this do it?

Maybe. Maybe Shannon was alone because she couldn't be alone. Alone because they wouldn't let her be. I would, he thought. All you would have to do is love me, Shannon. That's all, and you would never be alone again. You would never have to sit at your window again and stare outside and wonder if you are loved. Never.

Because I love you, you would love me.

And the Shannon in his mind smiled.

A knock came then, on his door. Mom.

"Dinnertime, Georgie. Are you working on your homework?"

He sat up suddenly and lied. "Yeah."

"Well, come on."

The screen had settled into the repeating pattern of his screensaver and blinked briefly as he shut it off. It was dim in the bedroom now; only a little light streamed through the shades of his window and it took a few seconds for his eyes to adjust. He looked back at his knapsack and went over to it, pulled out a textbook and left it open on his bed. There was a danger that after dinner Mom or Dad would volunteer to help and he had to have something to back up his lie.

It was brighter in the dining room, lit by the two big bulbs of the lamp that hung over the table. Dad sat there with the newspaper in front of him, reading. Mom was in the kitchen and as she emerged with the plates Georgie walked to his place and sat.

Dad looked up. "Hello, son."

"Hi."

"How was your day?"

Georgie fidgeted. Just his luck. Usually Dad was quiet at dinner and minded his own business, but once in a while he got it into his head that they needed to talk, that it was good for the family or something. Georgie shrugged his shoulders.

"Okay."

"How's school?"

"Fine."

"What are you studying?"

"Math."

Dad chuckled and took a bite of his meal. "I was pretty good at math in my day," he said. "How about I take a look at it with you?"

"That's all right. I'm doing okay at it."

Mom sat and watched them. She was a heavy woman, her weight less from eating too much than from a lack of exercise. She had a tired look to her too, distant sometimes, as though life had been unexpectedly hard, as though there was some hidden disappointment there that she had never found. Now her eyes narrowed and she turned to her son.

"You had a D on your last test, Georgie."

Georgie shrank a bit in his chair. "That was a week ago," he said. "I'm studying harder now."

"Then your father can help you study. After dinner."

There was a tone of finality in her voice that sundered his resistance. Georgie looked over at his father, who smiled.

"It's not easy at your age," the man said as he chewed. "I know, believe me. But these aren't the old days when hard work was enough. Now it's just a part of things; you've got to be smart, and you've got to go after what you want. Nobody's going to give anything to you in life."

"So how do you get it?" Georgie asked. He was being sarcastic but Dad didn't notice.

"You've got to be better than the next guy. Smarter, tougher." The man grinned at him. "You've got to find the new angle on things, Georgie. Figure out a better way to do it. Use your brain and think things through."

Georgie nodded and tried to look as though he cared. It wasn't easy; nor was the speech original. Dad had a way of talking about life that Georgie had heard before and as they finished dinner and rose he went on with it, even as Georgie went for his knapsack and laid it out on the dining room table.

Dad stopped for a moment as he sat. He spoke again.

"You still follow the game?" he asked.

Georgie blinked in surprise. He nodded.

"How's your Shannon doing?"

Georgie reddened. This was secret stuff, something Dad wouldn't understand. It wasn't his business, either. Georgie spoke softly.

"She's doing okay, I guess."

"Still undefeated?"

"Yeah."

"That's good. She's your girl, isn't she?"

Georgie looked down, tried to shrug. "Yeah, sure. I guess so."

The man chuckled, reached out and ruffled Georgie's hair a bit. "All right," he said. "Let's see what you've got. Algebra? Tough stuff. I remember it, though. You'd be amazed at how useful this will be someday."

Georgie nodded. "Dad?" he asked.

"Uh-huh?"

"Can you be lonely with people around you?"

Dad looked at him. Georgie felt a flash of shame, that he had asked something stupid, that Dad would laugh. But Dad only paused and when he spoke his tone was gentle.

"I suppose that depends."

"On what?"

"Who you are. Most people like having other people around them."

"Friends and stuff?" asked Georgie.

"Friends, family. People you care about."

Georgie looked down at his textbook, picked up his pencil and rolled it between his fingers. Dad spoke again.

"What are you getting at, Georgie?"

With a shrug, Georgie rolled the pencil again. "Just wondering," he said. "What if people are with you all the time?"

"Too much of a good thing isn't a good thing," Dad answered. "Everyone needs time to themselves. Some people like more of it than others. Know what I mean?"

He smiled at Georgie, and Georgie smiled back.

"Yeah."

"All right. Now tell me about algebra."

Georgie lay in bed later and stared up in the dim light at his poster. Shannon looked down at him as he did, her eyes and smile unmoving. He thought again of her, high in her room, alone. It made sense now. Like dying of thirst in the middle of the ocean. She was alone, his Shannon, despite everyone, because of everyone.

And something seemed different.

Not in her but in him. There was something new, a sensation he had never felt before, almost a notion he had never considered. A change in how things seemed, how he looked at her picture. He tried, lying there, to define it, to understand just what it was, but he could not.

Something, though.

Chapter 5

Days passed and matches passed. She played and she won and the world was filled with her joy. But there was a difference now, a change from before, from Moscow, from Cairo, from Buenos Aires, from Sydney. It wasn't clear at first, wasn't obvious. But Shannon O'hea was a bright girl and she had a good sense of things and when she put her mind to something she usually got an answer.

It was not as though anything was really different, though. This was the world championship and that meant certain things, meant long hours looking over the tactics of your competitors, meant answering questions for reporters and squinting under the hot glare of the camera lights.

Just like before.

Almost. Maybe. Maybe she was older now, and that meant things had changed. There was her body, strange sometimes, changing, growing. New feelings inside, new sensations. And she wondered as she looked at herself in the mirror if it was only her body, if maybe the new feelings were in her brain too, making her think different things.

"Mother?" she asked one day.

"Yes, dear?"

"Am I different?"

Mother looked at her for a moment. "Of course. You're very special."

"No...I mean different from the way I used to be."

Mother's tone changed, just a bit. "You're growing up, Shannon," she said. "You're becoming a young woman. Things change inside you then, and things outside seem different. But you're still Shannon."

"Do other people treat you different then?"

"Yes. Especially men."

Shannon nodded. Maybe that was it.

And maybe not.

She thought more about it.

Nothing was different but something was. As the first week of prelims ended with another spate of interviews over her four victories Shannon smiled and answered and nodded or shook her head and everyone saw.

Everyone knew. She pondered this, alone now, in her room. She was different, changing. She could see it in the slow budding of her breasts, in the changes in her groin, in how her hips were a bit wider now. But that was not it; not really, not at all. Those changes were, in truth, nothing different. No, the changes were outside her, in the others. In everyone. Every man and woman and child knew her, knew of her. They saw her soul when she played and they probed the rest of her when she didn't.

There. In front of her all the time and she had never seen it before.

Too obvious to notice, too much a part of her life to see easily.

Because it *was* impossible to talk in public and not have someone hear. It *was* impossible to touch her hair or scratch at her nose and not have someone see. She was Shannon O'hea and for some reason this meant that her words were valuable, that where she sat and what she ate and how she dressed were recorded on the cameras and microphones and beamed all over the world to people she would never meet. She thought back and she knew it had been this way at championships since she had won at Sydney and her behavior in public had grown into second nature.

Smile, wave, say something nice.

We think you are perfect so you must act as though you are. That's part of it, you know.

Part of it.

Part of The Game.

And more. Shannon went to bed that night, pulled the covers close around her neck. More than the game. Do you remember, how it was in those years? Intersect wasn't just a game anymore, was it? A game is a competition, with yourself or someone else. You practice, you play, you win or you lose and that's the end of it. The game is only as serious as the effort you put into it, only as meaningful as you decide it should be. It can be a lot or a little, a passing afternoon or a lifetime pursuit, but that's all it is.

For the Shannons, the Alicias, the Tanyas.

It is those who do not play that make it more. They do not stand under the bright lights, face the acclaim or the disdain, weep with the pain of a victory just missed or the joy of final, lifetime triumph. They do not know these things but they can sense them, just a bit. And from that sensing they build up the game, the sport, the things that you feel, and they make them more than they are and you more than you are.

You are more than an athlete, more than a performer. If you win you are perfect, somehow qualified to judge shoes or entertainment or styles of clothing or food or beer. For some reason they listen to your advice on things you know less about than they do.

But they listen, and they demand you speak.

Look at the vids. The local talk show. Remember? Watch it again and watch Shannon closely. Remember Moscow and then try to tell me that nothing had changed.

They took Shannon, Alicia, Tanya and Maria to the local vid station. It was to be a live broadcast and tickets for the studio audience were raffled for charity. Then that day the show was going to be rebroadcast three times. A crowd had gathered outside the building and local police were called out to keep them back. There was a sensation in the air as the four girls emerged from the limousine.

Look! Look!

Their Matrons guided them into dressing rooms. The producer had asked that they wear their Intersect uniforms and now they changed quickly before moving to the makeup station. The host appeared; he was a heavyset man with thinning, gray hair that he compensated for with an expensive hairpiece. He extended a hand to each of them.

"It's an honor, ladies. Thank you. Thank you."

The floor director appeared. "We'll need you in five," she said. "We've got the full hour; commercials every fifteen minutes." She extended earpieces to Maria and Tanya. "Instant translation through an interpreter in master control. Just answer normally. Understand?"

Tanya stuck the thing in her ear, waited, nodded. Maria did likewise.

They escorted them onstage, did some last minute checks on the lighting and microphones. Tanya's Matron said something to her in Russian and she nodded. The woman moved away.

"Keying up," the director said. "On my countdown." She hit zero and the lights came slowly on. The host burst into his monologue.

"Good morning! I'm Hugh Bradley and this is Chicago Talk. We've got a special show today and some special young ladies. I'm sure you know that the world Intersect championships are being held here in the windy city..."

He went on, introduced each of them to choreographed applause. There was a glass of water on his desk and he took a sip of it.

"Shannon O'hea. You're our reigning champion, aren't you?"

"Yes," Shannon said.

"Three times in a row, so far, yes?"

"No. I was third in Buenos Aires three years ago."

"But you want to make it three in a row this year, don't you?"

"I'm going to try."

He smiled, looked over at the others. "I suppose you girls have something to say about that, don't you? Tanya, you were second last year and a lot of people say you're getting better all the time. You have a lot of fans in Russia, don't you?"

Tanya answered yes.

"Fan clubs? We have them here, you know. In fact I can see in our audience we have a few representatives. Let's give them a hand!"

The lights went on in the studio, illuminating the applauding crowd. Shannon scanned the faces there. Old and young, male and female, black and white and brown. They went to a commercial and she found herself watching the crowd closely. There was a girl in the front row, the shape of her face obscured a bit behind thick glasses and long hair. Shannon centered on her, unmoving, and found the girl staring back.

"Welcome! If you've just tuned in, I'm Hugh Bradley and this is Chicago Talk. We've got some real champions here today..."

The lights faded a bit and the girl, dimmer now but visible, raised a finger to push her glasses back on her face.

Shannon found herself drinking in every motion.

"Can you tell us a bit about yourself, Shannon? What is it you like to do when you're not in the network? Any special hobbies?"

She looked back at the host. "Nothing special," she said. "I've been lucky because I love to travel."

"Do you have a special pet, maybe a goldfish? I had a goldfish when I was young."

"We have a dog, back in Arizona."

"Ah. You're from Tucson, aren't you?"

"Yes."

"And you, Alicia. You're from Baltimore?"

Alicia nodded. "Yes. I was born there."

"And Maria? What city in Brazil do you come from?"

A second's wait for the translator and then: "Belo Horizonte."

"How do you like America, Maria?"

Shannon looked back at the crowd. The girl was still there, staring. She had on a printed blouse and new pants, and her hair had been recently combed. Her mouth had come open, just slightly, as though she had a cold and her nose was stuffed.

What is it you do? Shannon wondered suddenly. Who are you?

A commercial break came and went. Tanya talked about Moscow, about her family's apartment and how they had such a nice Dacha in the country where she and her father picked mushrooms in the off season.

"Alicia, it's well known that you and Shannon are good friends. Do you think this will affect how you compete?"

"We're scheduled to meet in the next round of prelims," Alicia said.

"Is that right? That should be a match to watch. Any predictions, Shannon?"

Shannon shook her head. "No."

He looked surprised, hesitated for a second. "How about you, Alicia?"

"No. None."

He turned to Maria and asked her something. Shannon blinked. The girl in the audience had not moved, not budged. What are you looking at? Shannon thought suddenly. What's so special? The empty face gave no answer and Shannon tried to look away.

And failed. This is clear on the old vid. Look at it, just at that moment. Shannon wasn't watching Hugh Bradley, not at all, and you can see on his face that this bothered him. She was looking out instead, out and away.

They adjusted the camera angles because it was live and they couldn't coach her. The distraction was less evident then and from Shannon's eyes there was no clue as to what it was she saw.

Much less what she thought.

Shannon stared. The girl stared. There is no indication that she ever knew what was happening, that she ever suspected that Shannon had fixed on her. In truth we don't even know who she was.

"Shannon, you've got a lot of fans. A lot of people look up to you. Is there anything you'd like to tell them?"

She hesitated, blinked. The other girls watched her too, waiting.

"Just thank you," she said. "For everything."

"You're young. You're pretty. You're a champion. Is it ever hard, dealing with all that?"

Now Shannon looked down, at her feet. She raised her head again and spoke softly. "I do miss my dad sometimes, and my brother."

"Would you like to say hello to them? Tell them you love them?"

"They know."

The girl had shifted, crossed her legs. And Shannon began wondering to herself just then, wondering and thinking and building on it. What if I was suddenly you? No more Shannon O'hea, just you, watching and dreaming and not knowing that I'm not so perfect, that we're not so different, you and I. What would it be like to get up from your seat at the end of the hour and walk out of here without being followed and guarded and photographed? Maybe go home to a house and a family and put on an old pair of jeans and play outside? Just be you instead of me?

Could we meet? You could tell me what it's like, being you and not having people worship everything you say. You could be honest and see that I'm more than the interviews and the matrices and the game.

The girl's eyes brightened suddenly and she smiled.

The smile of the faithful and the damned.

And Shannon had to look away.

"We're almost out of time, I'm afraid," the host said. "Shannon, is there anything you'd like to say to America?"

She tensed. "Again?"

"What do you have to say to America, Shannon?"

She paused, concentrated. Old reflex came in.

"I'm very happy to be here."

He asked the others too, closed with a pitch for his show and the sport. Shannon stayed very still as the lights faded, watching her hands on her lap. Then it was busy as the crew moved over the set, disconnecting microphones and moving props, talking back and forth as they did.

"Shannon?"

It was her Matron. Shannon rose and walked with her off the set.

It was a quiet ride back to the hotel.

Prelims resumed tomorrow. Two matches: Da Zi Zhen and Alicia. Shannon thought of Moscow and wondered now about what Alicia had asked and what she had said. It was an important match but still only a prelim, and it shouldn't have bothered her so, but it did.

They ate before the cameras, smiled. Tanya proposed a toast to good health and they raised their glasses of water and juice to it. Then it was out, a few at a time, up to the elevators and the rooms, away from the billion eyes and million questions.

Up to peace in their guarded rooms.

Shannon sat at her window for some time, staring out at the black sky and the dark form of the lake beneath it. It was peaceful and silent here, high above the din of the city. A few faint stars were visible, flickering in the haze, and they made her think of home.

Home.

A place she barely knew. She thought back again without meaning to. Michelle, Rose, Lisa. What had they looked like? What had they done together? What had they thought when she had moved away, into her new life? What did they think now, when they saw her on the network?

Look! We knew her! She was our friend, they might say.

Or they might not. Shannon looked around, at the room, at the big, comfortable bed and the large-screen vid and the closet full of fine clothes. Stuff her old friends might well envy.

Had she abandoned them for these things?

Shannon O'hea was a hard little girl. Life in Intersect had made her so. It had given her poise and a sharp, analytical mind that most adults would envy. But no game and no life can entirely make up for the experience of years, and it was an absolute truth that Shannon O'hea was still a thirteen year old and that there was a part of her that knew she was not ready for any of this.

And she knew as well that the girl in the audience would have given anything to trade places with her. But you don't know, do you? she thought. You think it's worth it, all of it, to be envied and rich and pretty and to have strange men and women pushing their way into photographs with you? But what's it worth to walk down the street alone? What's it worth to go outside and just look like you, not like someone people want to see?

Shannon sighed, rubbed at her brow. It was because of the girl in the studio, of the girls in the crowd at the magtrain station, and the girls at the airports in Sydney, Buenos Aires, Cairo and Moscow. She envied them suddenly, knowing in that moment how each of them felt, how each of them yearned for something that could not be. It was a gulf, this envy, a vast canyon neither could cross. It occurred to Shannon then that perhaps she did not know what it was she envied, either, any more than they did.

Did they understand that to be perfect is impossible?

Did she understand what it was like to be flawed, to be fat or ugly or stupid? Did she know that pain? Could she?

She went to the mirror, stared into it. What was it about this face that made it beautiful? It had eyes, a nose, a mouth. Cheeks and cheekbones and eyebrows and hair. Lips around the mouth, teeth below. She made a face, screwed her features into as grotesque a parody as she could. Would they find that beautiful too? Would the women envy this and would men watch her the way some of them did, with that faint touch of lust in their eyes? What if she were scarred, burned?

She relaxed. The parody vanished.

"It's just a face," she said to herself. "I don't understand."

And it's just a game, too.

She pulled on a robe, stepped from her room. The walk was short this time, just a short stretch down the hall. Alicia answered quickly as she knocked.

"Hi."

Shannon smiled. "Busy?"

Alicia shook her head. "We were just finishing," she said, and stepped back. Behind her, her Matron rose from a chair. Alicia turned to her as Shannon stepped inside the door. "Can you come back?" she asked.

The woman watched Shannon and nodded. "Half an hour," she said. "You need your sleep." She stepped out the door and closed it behind her.

Alicia went to her bed and sat down. Shannon took the chair. "The reporters would lose it if they knew you were here," Alicia said.

"The match?"

"Yeah. I'm glad you came, though. Em isn't much fun during tournaments."

"She's a Matron. They're not supposed to be fun."

Alicia chuckled, glanced over at the small refrigerator by the room's empty bar.

"You want some ice cream? I had them send some up last night. If you turn the cool all the way up it doesn't melt."

"Sure."

Alicia rose and opened the refrigerator door, took out a big cup. She reached for two spoons from the bar. "No bowls," she said. "Sorry."

"It's okay," Shannon answered, moving to the bed.

They sat cross-legged, the cup between them, and ate. The ice cream wasn't hard like a real freezer would make it, but soft and easy to spoon. Alicia scooped up a mass of the stuff, licked at it.

"Good?"

Shannon nodded.

"This is probably going to make us fat. No more talk shows."

"Too bad." Shannon took a large bite, smiled.

Alicia smiled too.

They ate, too much probably, as kids will do. It wasn't long before Shannon hit the bottom of the cup. She looked up at her friend.

"Alicia, what are we doing?"

"Huh?"

"Here, I mean. In Chicago."

"Competing. Aren't we?"

"I don't know."

Alicia watched her for a few seconds. "Shannon, are you all right?"

Shannon looked away, set her spoon in the cup. "Never mind," she said. "Stupid question."

Alicia took the cup, turned in her place and set it on the table by her bed. She faced Shannon again, rested her chin in her hands.

"You talking about the game?" she asked.

"Yeah."

"I guess we play, we win, we lose."

Shannon shook her head. "No. It's more than that. I don't know what."

"You don't think we'll be friends after tomorrow?"

She had thought of that, briefly. She had thought about Moscow and she had wondered what would have happened if they had played. How would Alicia have felt, if Shannon had torn her apart the way she did Tanya Kirilova? Perhaps that was why she had come, to spend one last time with Alicia before they began to hate one another. She looked at Alicia, looked hard until her friend glanced away. She looked at her features, her hair, the way her body was shaped. And Shannon knew it was more than that. The reporters and the fans and even the Matrons might expect them to be enemies but these people were far away from how it felt to be an Intersect girl.

"They don't think so," she said, cocking her head towards the door.

Alicia sighed. "I think they're wrong. Who else have we got to be friends with?"

Shannon scratched at her scalp. "That's true."

Alicia lay back, uncrossed her legs, stared up at the ceiling. "I keep thinking about things," she said.

"Things?"

"Like what's going to happen when we can't compete anymore? I keep thinking about that. What are we going to do?"

Shannon shrugged her shoulders. She had never given this much thought; Intersect was her life and had been for years. That there was anything else to do had seldom occurred to her.

She thought of the chasm again. What did other, normal people, do with their lives?

"I don't know," she said.

Alicia paused. Then she said, "I don't talk to my Pop. All he wants is a world championship. My mom doesn't like me seeing you but she can't say anything. Everything's the game to them."

"You don't like Intersect?"

"Oh, I do. It's the only thing I've ever been any good at."

Shannon nodded. "Me too."

"What if we have to be good at something else when we get older?"

This time Shannon said nothing, and soon Alicia's Matron returned with a firm knock on the door. They returned the cup to the refrigerator and let her in. Shannon said goodnight and returned to the hall, walking slowly back to her room. She had a thought then, an elaboration on her secret fantasy. Go to the elevator, go down, vanish into obscurity rather than face Alicia in the game and destroy her. Leave the game behind. Leave behind the expectations and become mundane, normal.

Have friends that stay.

But Shannon knew better than all this; she knew herself and the world well enough to know that running will not let you escape what others make you out to be.

Someday, though. Just maybe.

Chapter 6

▼

They aired the show three times, as promised. Georgie watched it all three times and recorded it twice to be sure he had it. One copy he hid in his closet and the other under his mattress. He could feel the one copy as he sat on his bed, just a faint bump from the disc case, a little reminder that a bit of Shannon O'hea was close, that close.

Oh Shannon, he thought. You're so far away. Please come to me…

She did, in the matrices. Maybe that was what made the game so good. She did come to you, as she played; all of them did. To watch Alicia was to watch a wonder, and Tanya was so perfect, so precise. Mom and Dad knew this too, and the Joneses, and the Riveras, and they watched as Georgie watched, in their VR chairs, and they could not help but talk about it afterward, just like he and Jim and Adam did.

"Great move. Made me feel young."

"That Shannon is quite something, isn't she?"

"Who thought this game up in the first place? Greatest damn invention ever made."

Georgie would listen as they talked, smile. The game was good; good to you, good for you. That's what everyone was saying, really. Have your cake and eat it too. More now, though. Dad would come to him when Shannon won, smile and gently squeeze his shoulder as though congratulating him.

"She's a fine girl, your Shannon. Fine."

And Georgie would nod, a bit embarrassed, and say nothing. Dad would go on then, about responsibility, about how Shannon was smart, too, about how she always studied, about how she would be quite something even after she grew too old for Intersect. Georgie wondered a lot about how Dad knew this and why it was so important for him to tell him.

Never mind. They were right about one thing: Intersect was the greatest thing ever, and Shannon was the best part of that.

He had a book on Intersect and it had her bio and a picture. It was dated now but that was all right; he pulled it from his desk and it fell open to her. With a smile he read.

Born August 23. San Francisco. Moved to Arizona when she was five. Father works as a maintenance engineer; mother worked as a paralegal before Shannon entered competition full time. One brother, Leonard.

Leonard. Maybe someday he would meet Leonard and the two of them would get along just fine.

So you like my sister, do you?
Oh yes, she's a fine girl. Truly.
I'm glad you take such good care of her, Georgie.
Leonard, yes. They would be good friends.

Georgie stared at the book for some time, at the pictures. He read the article again but it was somehow not quite enough.

Ah. Now he had better.

He got up, moved to the bed, took out the disc from under the mattress. The screen on his computer was small, not like the one in the living room that Mom watched, but it was private and it would do. He turned it on, plugged in the earphones, slid in the disc. As the program started he reclined with a smile.

"Good morning! I'm Hugh Bradley and this is Chicago Talk. We've got a special show today and some special young ladies. I'm sure you know that the world Intersect championships are being held here in the windy city..."

The camera panned back and Georgie leaned forward again to get a closer look at the screen. The words faded and became nothing; the host faded; the other girls faded. Just Shannon, shimmering slightly, her eyes off the camera, somewhere.

"Georgie?"

He snapped up, paused the vid.

Mom, at the door.

"Georgie?"

He felt his eyes narrow slowly. "What?"

"Georgie, what are you doing?"

"Nothing. Watching some vid."

"Vid? Is your homework done?"

He lied. "Yeah."

"Can I see it?"

She had her dangerous voice on, the one that meant that she knew what he knew. He responded slowly.

"Why?"

"I want to be sure it looks nice."

"It's not quite finished."

"You just said it was."

"It will be. I just needed a break."

She should have backed off now. Usually she did. But instead she stepped inside the room and stood very close.

"Chicago Talk again?" she asked, and he saw her look over at the poster of Shannon.

"I like the show."

"You never watched it before today."

He scratched at the back of his head. "I just needed a break," he repeated.

She leaned over him, punched at the eject button on the computer. The disc popped out and she took it. "I want your homework done, Georgie," she said. "You can have this back when it is."

"But Mom…"

"No, Georgie."

He watched her as she stepped out the door, leaving it open behind her. Out in the living room he heard his father, a bit of low mumbling. It was about him, he knew, and Shannon. He'd heard them before.

Not healthy. Maybe he's getting too involved with the game.

There's worse things he could get into, you know.

Still, he seems obsessed sometimes.

They all are at that age. Weren't we?

Georgie went back to his homework, sat at his desk and applied himself. It was hard but not that hard and he knew his mother; if he got it done he would get his disc back and if there was time he could get another look at Shannon before he went to bed. But he wondered too, as he worked and as he read, how they could love the game so much and expect him not to.

And anyway, he said to himself, I'm not obsessed any more than they are.

Oh yes. He was lying. It's obvious in hindsight, like so many things are. But this was not a simple lie about Georgie's homework; no, it was a fundamental lie that is universal.

A lie in all of us.

You can try and deny it, of course. You can say that you're calm and collected and rational and that you control your sex drive and your emotions and your spirituality. It's easy.

To say.

And that's what we all do. Like Georgie, we say. Like Georgie, we claim. And like Georgie, we lie.

Can you see yourself honestly? Can anyone?

Look at the human animal and you will see two parts, two faces. One is the lie, a facade. It is the thing we show the world, the thing we want the world to see and much of it is also the thing we want to be. Perhaps you say to me: I am male. I am strong, in control. I am female. I am loving and compassionate. I am heterosexual and sane and honest and I know myself.

But beneath this facade is another you and this is the truth you seek to hide. It does more than claim its honesty; it *is* honest. It is the truth of who you are: each of your successes and failures, of the dark thoughts you are afraid of and the light you are not certain you have. It is all the good and all the evil of your soul and to deny it is to deny your own existence.

Do you?

Georgie did and so did Shannon. So did their parents and so did the sportscasters and the advertisers and all the billions who tuned in to watch the game. So did you and so did I, because that was the truth of Intersect.

The facade that we wanted to see.

Chapter 7

They brought them together from the hotel, sitting in the back of the limousine in their shiny warm-ups. They said little as they sat, as the car maneuvered down the lakeshore. It was windy today and the waves were choppy.

Out then, through the crowds, into the museum. Up the stairs past guards who smiled at them and at their Matrons. From there into the interface chambers.

This was a lonely place, the interface chamber; only a special VR chair, a little room to pace, a shelf in the wall with a pitcher of water and a few cups. Some girls brought Matrons here, or mothers or fathers, or a friend to relieve the tension. This was a private place and company a private choice; every girl was different and who you chose to have with you was considered sacrosanct.

Shannon was alone, though. She had always played alone. Alicia had her Matron to calm her with prattle.

Moments passed.

There is a feeling that comes when you are about to compete, or perform, or speak in public. Events become slow; seconds take minutes to unfold as your heart pounds against your ribs. This declines with age and experience but never entirely disappears, because to feel it is to know that suddenly you are at the center. Every action you make is scrutinized, judged. It is the time you have waited for, worked toward, concentrated on. It is easier when the competition or performance begins because then you are busy, but in the time just before you can do nothing but wait and think.

Half the battle is here.

Alicia was first, against Yombe Mchombo of Ethiopia. Shannon followed against Da Zi Zhen. Neither received much attention save for the purists and neither match produced any surprises. Alicia won and Shannon won.

They waited again. Alicia stepped out, went to the toilet. Shannon stared at the wall of her chamber. Across the way, Monique Armeneau beat little Julie West of Canada. The clock moved forward, bit by bit, and slowly at first and then more quickly people began to break away from their day, began to move to VR chairs and tune in. Hushed words went out across America: Our girls. Our best.

Shannon O'hea. Alicia Rinehart.

Juanita Gregorio beat Anna Solveg.

Oddsmakers favored Shannon, but only just. She rose, stretched, yawned. She had a way of concentrating on nothing before a match, of sitting and staring. It was difficult today, though. She kept thinking of Moscow.

The page chimed.

"O'hea. Rinehart."

Shannon climbed into the VR chair, made herself comfortable.

The chamber faded.

A rush greeted her; exact numbers meshed themselves with her thoughts, her feelings. She drew herself as a line, a plane, grounding herself in the beauty of geometry. She flexed and floated and prepared.

Across the way, she sensed Alicia.

Alicia was dancing. There was a beauty to it, a hypnotic sense to her digital pirouettes. A joy in being what she was, in interfacing and moving along the electronic paths of a supercomputer chip. Shannon hesitated, pulled back. In her pause there was grace, love, perfection. She built a construct of herself, a mirror image, and extended it into the maelstrom that was her friend.

Careful now, careful.

Alicia caught it, brought it close, spun it away with a laugh. Her spin widened, opened, bits of starlight flying out. Shannon blocked with an algorithm, a subsection of processing line, sent out a tendril of irrational numbers.

They sparred, parried. Time became numbers to be twisted. Alicia probed and found only the perfect wall of Shannon's beauty. Shannon lanced out but Alicia moved away, all grace.

All around the world the billions watched in awe. Twenty minutes passed and more people came, joined. This was no Moscow, no sudden victory. This was a match between masters, a one in a thousand match. Some who watched began to weep, to shiver; some left because it was more beauty than they could stand.

Feint with the infinity of pi. Redraw yourself as she erases what you were. Find the point and join.

Intersect.

Thirty minutes.

Dance, flex, move.

Intersect.

Forty minutes. Remember the title match between York and Naim?

Intersect.

Shannon saw it first. Not a mistake, not a flaw. Only a result; small but undeniable, indefensible. A result fixed in absolute logic, in the way she and Alicia meshed here, in the combinations they had formed. She saw it and knew it and in that moment could only watch.

Alicia would win.

One by one Shannon's walls fell. One step at a time she retreated.

And Alicia danced.

Too perfect, now. She danced and it was the essence of the game, the perfect intersection. She was deep in the computers, spread among synapses and memory and processors. Shannon watched and the beauty of it overcame her; she could feel herself rising, out now, out. Out with love and joy and defeat.

Out into the comfort of her VR chair, into tears and the empty chamber.

Alicia! they cried. Upset! Upset! Suddenly there was no Shannon O'hea, no defending champion, no beautiful angel to follow with cameras. No, there was Alicia instead, who danced in the matrices and who had upset the master.

It was only a prelim, someone reminded.

Yes, but is it the future? O'hea isn't scheduled for another match till Tuesday. Will she lose her composure? For a moment there was a pause, a hesitation. Cameras zoomed in and stayed on the doors of the Museum of Science and Industry.

Waiting.

Were you watching then? Did you see her as she emerged?

Shannon! the reporters cried. Shannon! What do you have to say? What went wrong?

America is watching, Shannon. You owe us an answer.

The vids are clear. Shannon said nothing. Not a word, not a whisper. Only a look that left us angry and shocked. A look that was not Shannon O'hea, but someone else, someone we didn't know.

Someone who had been crying.

Yes. The perfect girl was not so perfect after all.

What a baby, someone said. This isn't a sport for the weak, you know.

Oh, but Alicia! How she shone!

Watch out, Tanya, America's got a new champion!

Do you remember? How the tide shifted, if only for a little while? How Alicia's performance had been so perfect that we passed Shannon by?

Most people do.

Of Shannon's flaws we can say this: they were there before and they were there after. If you've seen the vids you can tell she had been weeping; but do you know why? Most of us never asked, lost in our dreams. But it was not defeat that made Shannon weep, not suffering. Such things could not be, just then, not for her, not for anyone. She had seen Alicia's dance and had bathed in its joy. Can you blame her for weeping then? Why was she not allowed to share in the joy and love of her friend? That she did not want to talk after the match is understandable—who did, after all?

Shannon slid into her limousine, closed the door, and buried her head in her hands. They went straight back, along the lakefront and into the hotel. Security was there, waiting, and they cordoned off the lobby as she went through.

Up to the high, private floor of the north tower.

Mother met her there. Shannon stepped inside her room and walked to the bed and sat down. Mother watched her for a time, then moved to her side.

"Shannon?" she asked.

Shannon did not speak and Mother grew just a bit afraid. For there was a circle of the mothers in this game, bound by the same sort of threads that bound their daughters: commonality and envy and respect. But the mothers were older, too, and they saw much that the world did not.

Risks, for example.

Not sabotage, not cheating. These were nearly impossible to carry off. But other things, things whispered, watched for, feared.

"Shannon?"

"Yes, Mother?"

"I saw the match. You did the best you could."

Shannon nodded. She did not move and her mother put an arm around her.

"You're going to come back, you know. I think—"

"Please, Mother," Shannon said. "Not now."

The woman nodded. "Would you like anything? I could have them send up dinner."

"No."

"All right." Mother was silent then, for a time.

Shannon stared at her feet, wiggled a toe and saw the material of her shoe flex with the motion. There was something odd here, very odd, but she didn't quite know what it was. Something in the air that had not been there before.

Or maybe it was in her.

She did not move.

Mother rose eventually, went to do something. When she returned she knelt before her daughter.

"Shannon, are you all right?"

"I don't know."

Mother felt fear again, wiggling deep inside.

"Do you want me to get a doctor?"

"No. It's not that." And Shannon looked up, watched her mother closely.

Mother watched her back, extended a hand and caressed her knee. Shannon spoke again, her voice so small it was almost a whisper.

"Mother, I don't know how I'm supposed to feel."

"What do you mean?"

Shannon looked around her, at the hotel room, the bed, the painting of a lighthouse on the wall, the large mirror beside it. The bouquet of flowers by the vid, sent by the mayor.

"About this," she said.

"I don't understand."

Shannon didn't either, really. It was a strange sensation inside her but not one that formed readily into words. She closed her eyes and saw the thing that was Alicia, dancing on each matrix. She saw and then once again she felt the beauty of her friend, spinning in mathematical perfection.

Breaking her own constructs down, driving her into defeat. Shannon had never done what Alicia did today. It was a style thing, of course, at least in part. But there was more too. Something about Alicia that made the constructs and the theorems sing, something that was not in Shannon and that would never be in Shannon. A unique beauty that was Alicia.

And there it was.

Shannon opened her eyes. Mother was still there, watching.

There it was, because it wasn't. Shannon searched herself, looked deep inside for the dark kernel of envy that she should have felt. Envy, yes. Envy of her friend, for the attention, for the skill, for the beauty that would forever be associated with the time Alicia the dancer beat the champion Shannon O'hea. And after she had looked and looked and pondered for a moment Shannon tried to create this envy, to call it forth like an old friend.

Even there she failed.

"Mother," she said again, "I don't know how I'm supposed to feel."

Mother squeezed her knee. "Shannon, you *will* come back. You're going to beat this girl at her own game."

Shannon looked down at the woman's hand, placed her own over it. Then she rose and Mother stood too, and Shannon walked over to the mirror and stared into her reflection. And she said, "Does it matter, really?"

It did, of course, to some.

Alicia emerged later, her Matron at her side. There was a smile on her face, a triumph, because she of all people knew what she had done and how perfect it had been. The reporters were there, still stung by Shannon, wanting attention as all reporters really do deep inside, waiting for Alicia the dancer, the new queen.

There! Yes!

Alicia, how do you feel?

"Fine."

The setup move, just before the end; did you plan it that way?

"Not completely. It just felt right."

God, yes. It did.

Did you think you had a chance when you came into this match?

Alicia hesitated here, just for a second. And then she nodded.

"Yeah."

An old reporter spoke then. He was gray, his suit matching his hair, his face lined with experience and age. He asked what everyone was thinking.

"Alicia, what do you think of Shannon now that you've beaten her? What do you think of your friendship?"

This sank in. Alicia looked down at her feet and the smile was gone. She shook her head, whispered something that missed the mike.

"What was that, Alicia?" asked the old reporter.

She whispered again, still looking down. This time the mike caught it.

"I don't know."

She went then. There were other matches to be held and they needed the room. She stepped to the waiting limousine, opened the door and got inside. As it closed the reporters began talking again.

Shannon, crying. Can you believe it?

Bad sport, I'd say. Can dish it out but can't take it.

Envious little bitch.

Everything changed. Predictions were reforecast, odds shuffled around. The experts ignored the fact that Shannon had won all her other matches, that she was still among the top seeds. Those were numbers, bound by rules, and rules are the first things to go when excitement sets in.

Especially when you saw the match firsthand from a VR chair.

But who can say what Alicia saw? Who can testify how she felt, watching the reporters and the Matrons and the other girls? Because she watched, you know, when she emerged from the museum. She heard and she did feel it as they cut Shannon down, as they praised her at Shannon's expense. There was a certain joy in them as they did, and she saw this as she answered them.

How does it feel to have beaten the World Champion, Alicia?

How does it feel?

It had to happen. That Shannon—too perfect, if you ask me. Headed for a fall. What do you think, Jeff?

I think what I've always thought: Intersect girls can't be friends. I said it in Moscow and I'll say it here.

This is the best thing that could have happened to Alicia. A real competitor's got no room for friends, not in this sport. I see a real future for Alicia now.

They didn't see, of course, the reality of now. In the reality of now Alicia was holding on for dear life because with every word she heard she knew that this was not right. Look at the vid and see her face. Rigid, hard, until that last second when she is climbing into the limo.

Her mother was there and she hugged her close.

"Oh, dear, I'm so happy!"

They drove up the lakeshore. It was late in the day and a cold wind rocked the trees gently. Alicia sat and her face relaxed and she scratched at her head. Her mother stroked her hair.

"I think tonight you need to dress up for dinner. I'll have someone come up and fit you."

She went on, still stroking her daughter's hair, as the car pulled into the hotel garage. Alicia did not move for a moment, then rose, stepped out into the public eye again.

And she watched as the reporters surged forward. She stared at them as they thrust microphones through the wall of security men, as they shouted questions at her. She did not answer, remember? Have you ever wondered why?

Have you ever been alone?

She wanted to cry. As the elevator doors opened she wanted to rush down the hall and beat on Shannon's door and beg her friend not to leave her. Because she could not help but believe what they all were saying now, that there could be no friends in the game, that Intersect girls destroyed each other, ripped each other down.

Have you ever been afraid?

She and her mother and her Matron went on to her room, closed and locked the door. Her mother called for service, went to the closet and began thumbing through dresses. Her Matron sat silently and watched her.

Have you ever been unsure?

Alicia sat and watched her mother. And it became clear to her then, growing for the first time, that she would never again be just somebody, just one of the many contenders. She was a favorite now, a force to be watched in the game.

But this did not make her happy.

For all these thoughts melded into one as she sat. All these thoughts bonded together until they were the one thought, the one that had begun in Moscow, that had built from that seed, that moment when she had been alone and a stranger had knocked quietly on her door.

Dinner.

They were ready to rip Shannon apart when it finally came. Some hoped she wouldn't come at all, that they could write stories about the bitter champion past her prime, hiding up in her room and clinging to past glories. How wrong we were, they wanted to say, to call Shannon O'hea our golden girl, to praise the beauty of her soul, to make her a goddess.

They waited at the press table like hungry cats, ready for the kill. Will she cry again? someone asked. Intersect girls are never friends and this is why. It should have happened in Moscow; watch their eyes as they cut each other apart. Will they sit together now?

Oh, I hope so.

Yes, I hope so.

Lights came on; cameras did likewise. The first of the girls arrived and the commentators smiled in anticipation.

And they were not prepared for what followed.

Monica Chavez and Li Yon, gliding, sitting. Tanya Kirilova, austere. Fatima Al-Hakim, so shy, and Amanda Sawyer and Maria Chavez and one more and one more until then, from the elevator, Alicia.

Alone save for her Matron. The cameras followed, the hushed voices spoke.

Where is her friend?

Have they fought? Have they spoken?

Ask her! Ask her!

A reporter dared to step forward, found himself face to face with the iron stare of Alicia's Matron. He backed away.

After dinner, then. Just wait.

Alicia sat. Watch the vids now: she says something to Tanya, and Tanya nods. Alicia looks around, her eyes wide, scanning. Look at those eyes sometime; there is something behind them about to break, something on the edge of a chasm, about to fall.

Something, perhaps, that is wondering if what she has given up is worth what she has gained.

But watch the vids, for there is more.

A sweep, suddenly, to the elevator. And there, in white, shining and beautiful, is Shannon O'hea. No words from anywhere as she moves forward, all lightness and grace. Not a sound, not a breath. A secondary camera catches Alicia and she is watching and her mouth is trying to form a bit of a smile, but she is afraid behind that smile and you can see it. Shannon moving forward, timeless perfection, no trace of a tear in her eye, passing Maria Chavez and just touching her as she passes, like a mother with her child. And a smile for Fatima Al-Hakim and a perfect nod to Li Yon, and then she is there and Alicia has risen without knowing why, to face her.

Watch.

Shannon extends her arms, reaches for Alicia. Alicia hesitates, trembles. Her mouth is just open and her eyes draw a picture of despair. And then Shannon embraces her, draws her close and holds her. Alicia is weeping now, her face visible and then buried in Shannon's bodice, weeping because she knows suddenly that it is all right, that it is just a game and that there is something more in the world.

Something that does not die.

Chapter 8

The game went on and now it captured the world's attention even more. Moscow was no fluke, we knew now. Shannon and Alicia are friends, real friends, see? This was a new dimension; Intersect was a lonely game but not for them. The matches themselves seemed to take on a new significance, a new power. Ratings rose and the angels battled with joy across an unreal but beautiful world. Tanya and Katherine Bent. Anna Solveg and Ellen Rodriguez. And the city watched and the world watched because we had seen in Shannon a new potential and we all wanted a piece of it.

Love we all could share.

And we wanted more.

Give it to me, Shannon. Move in the matrices and give what you gave to Alicia to me. Touch me as you touched Maria Chavez. Smile as you did to Fatima Al-Hakim.

But do it in the game where it is multiplied by a hundred, a thousand.

Preliminaries continued, began winding down. Remember Tanya against Tshering Dem?

Spin for me, Tanya.

Alicia against Monica Chavez?

Dance for me, Alicia.

Shannon against Li Yon?

Love for me, Shannon.

For me.

For me.

For me.

They had made it a habit to come here after school. Into the park and down the lakeshore, by the crowds that were sometimes gathered out in front of the Claremont Downtown. Jim and Adam and Georgie, pacing the afternoon away, talking about this match or about how Shannon or Alicia or Tanya looked last night on the vid. Sometimes they would catch a bus down to the Museum of Science and Industry and stand outside there with the people, just watching, imagining, remembering a match or hoping to see one of their favorites emerge and wave. On the weekend it was even better because they could do this all day, grabbing a hot dog from a vendor and eating it as they watched.

Monday. Wednesday. They had skipped Tuesday because Shannon had a match and they spent the afternoon in their VR chairs at home. On Thursday Jim had to get home so it was just Georgie and Adam. Alicia had a match that afternoon so they waited at the museum.

"This is cool," Adam said.

"Yeah," Georgie answered. He was a bit uncomfortable because he should have gone home too and he knew he was in for a lecture. Somehow, though, that didn't matter. There were priorities in life, things that were important and things that weren't.

A limousine pulled up to the museum and someone got in it. Alicia?

No. Someone else.

"I wonder sometimes," Adam said.

"Huh?"

"What it's like to play."

Georgie turned to his friend. "We can't play," he said. "You know that."

"Yeah." Adam nodded. He had a cola in his hand and sucked at the straw. "But what's it's like, I wonder."

"Sissy."

"Am not."

Georgie laughed. "It's supposed to be the best," he said. "Like heaven. They get what we get and more."

"Cool." Adam munched down on his hot dog and Georgie looked back at the museum. They were near the front of the crowd and he heard the sound around him as the doors opened up again and someone came out. He elbowed Adam.

"Alicia, dude!"

"Where?" Adam mumbled.

Georgie pointed. "There! There!"

And it was. The limousine appeared and she stepped down to it. The noise grew and people pressed forward. Policemen were there to stop them and clear a path as Alicia slid into the limo and the door closed behind her. Georgie could hear Adam beside him as the car moved away.

"Cool. Magnum cool."

"Yeah."

The crowd began to decompress, settling back from the police barricades. Adam had finished his hot dog and drink and he found a bin to drop the refuse into. Then he shoved his hands into his pockets and looked at Georgie.

"You wanna scope the hotel?" he asked.

Georgie nodded. They walked toward the lakefront, turned along the street to the bus stop. Adam said nothing as they boarded and the bus hurried north. When they got off he spoke.

"It must be cool."

"What?"

"To have everyone like you. To play the game and be famous. I wish we could play."

For a moment Georgie was silent and the only sounds were passing cars and their own footsteps. Then he said, "I like watching better."

"You wouldn't like to try it?"

Georgie had never thought about this and now he did. It wasn't easy, really. Intersect was a girl game and that was that. Girls played and guys watched. Everything about the game was expressed in the feminine: "she" and "her." *He* watched and *she* played. Georgie shuddered a bit, suddenly. What if Shannon wanted him to do something? What if he had to assemble constructs and theorems while she watched?

Would she judge him?

Would she love him?

Would he be alone?

His skin felt prickly all of a sudden. He spoke.

"I guess it would be neat."

Adam nodded. He grew quiet again, his hands forced deeply into his pockets and his head down, watching his feet as they moved. Georgie looked ahead, saw the facade of the Claremont. He didn't know what to say now, what to do. They were close to the hotel when Adam spoke again.

"Georgie?"

"Yeah."

"Don't tell what I said about wanting to play, okay? People would tease."

Georgie nodded. "All right. I won't."

"Swear it. They'll say I'm girly."

"I swear." Georgie watched his friend as they came to a stop and faced the hotel. It faced them back, its facade in shadow in the afternoon sun, silent, imposing. Georgie sighed, nodded again. It felt like there was some kind of weight to the air, something different. New and real and honest and mature. It was partly his promise to Adam, the responsibility it carried, and partly more and he wondered what this was.

The game, of course. But the game was different now, just a little bit, like it had been just a little bit different the other night as he lay in bed thinking. Different and strange and new and even frightening.

What does it mean? he wondered. They haven't changed anything—just a few more players this year, that's all. And how could that be bad anyway? More players, more matches. More time for the championship and that means more time to think about Intersect and watch it.

But what is it like to play? What's it like to be Shannon, or Alicia, or Tanya? Does wanting to know how they feel make me girly? He looked at Adam again as Adam watched the hotel. Georgie blinked, sighed.

Does being Shannon really mean being alone? Why didn't I see that before, last year or during the championship in Egypt? Maybe she wasn't alone then. Maybe I'm seeing something on the vid that wasn't there before, something in the way she looks at the camera.

Adam hadn't moved. He was standing very still and Georgie thought about his promise again. It was a piece of his friend he hadn't considered before, that maybe some boys might like to play, even though they couldn't. Fine; that's life. But the promise he had made was more. It was important because it wasn't just a kid thing. He knew this from the sound of his friend's voice, from the look in his eyes. Not a kid thing but a real thing, not a swear that you might break and then just say I'm sorry. A real swear, that to keep meant something more. Him, Georgie, something more, just like the game.

Growing, changing. Somehow less distant and more real, more tangible.

A piece of life that was more than just you and your VR chair.

Adam turned to him. "You thinking, Georgie?" he asked.

"Yeah."

"Okay." A pause and then, "You cool for the weekend? They're having a fair in Grant park. We could scope it and then come down here, see if anything's happening. Jim should be free too."

Georgie pulled his attention from the facade of the hotel, looked at his friend. "Yeah," he said. "That would be cool."

Chapter 9

Walk now, outside, into the streets, the parks. Watch as you do; who is it you pass? Do you know them? Can you look into their eyes and know their story?

Can you look into mine?

Yes and no.

For our stories and our lives are at once the same and unique. This is the paradox that makes us human. You know nothing of the stranger you pass yet there are some things you will always know.

There are dreams and ideas we all share.

Who am I? What makes me into me?

And what if I were you?

Some seek answers to these things.

Return now to Shannon. She was the stranger then, as the days passed and the prelims ended. We did not understand her though we should have. We should not have been surprised at her love for her friend and yet we were. But the love was only a part and we should have seen more.

Alone, she sat.

Alicia was at her final prelim. Mother was gone, out at something legal, negotiating an endorsement. And outside, the city beckoned.

What is it you see? What is it you believe about Shannon O'hea? Look harder, into what you recall. Only a part, yes?

Yes. For that is all we can ever see of another.

Shannon sat. Shannon thought. Shannon wondered.

This is why she rose again. Can you imagine her now? Can you think of what it was, to be her?

Why not? She thought it of you, that day.

Yes.

That was the day her Matron knocked gently on her door. Shannon let her in, walked to the window and stared out it.

"What is it?" she asked.

The woman remained expressionless. There isn't much to be said about her; the institution of the Matron was nearly as old as the game itself. The players were only children, and they were under stress and they were young and having another adult with them at tournaments helped keep them safe. Parents were not always rational about their little girls, after all. And Matrons were coaches, too; many were former players and the advice of a good Matron could win or lose a match. But a really good one also knew when to stay in the background. Shannon's Matron understood that Shannon made her own way in the game and that she was here only because the rules required it. Knowing this, the woman allowed it.

"There's a city fair this afternoon in Grant park," she answered. "The Chicago Symphony and some folk groups. Some of the other girls are going. I thought you might enjoy it."

Shannon turned. The room had a particular smell, a particular sense to it. Subtle, that. She watched the woman and then turned away.

"I'll think about it," she said.

"All right." The door closed and again Shannon was alone. She wrapped her arms tightly around herself, shivered.

To go meant being Shannon O'hea, meant being the World Champion and pandering to crowds. To stay meant being alone and still being Shannon O'hea.

She thought about Elena.

Intersect girl.

You.

And Alicia.

Shannon is not your friend, Alicia. She cannot be. She must compete, win, bring glory to America and The Game. Now you have defeated her and so you must hate her. And you must compete, win and bring glory. You, Alicia. You.

You, Shannon O'hea. You must hate Alicia for winning. You must prepare for the next match, must decide to destroy your friend.

Only there is more to Shannon O'hea, more to you.

What Elena didn't see.

Holding your friend close. Her face against your chest, pressing there, weeping. Afraid. So afraid that the tension fills the air like a taut string ready to snap. Afraid of you, for you, because of you. Alone, cut off.

Like you are.

Who knows? Who understands? Who sees?

Who stands for you?

Shannon opened her eyes and faced the city again. A bird passed by outside, quickly, on its way to somewhere. Down below, on the street, cars moved back and forth and out on the lake the triangular sail of a boat caught her eye.

Who stands for me?

She turned, moved to the dresser, reached into a drawer and pulled out an old pair of jeans. She changed into these and into a white blouse, pulled on a pair of sneakers and reached for her little purse and her coat.

At the mirror by the door she paused, inhaled deeply. And somehow she knew.

They had a bus for the group of them. Security men too, with long coats to cover their weapons and scanners, and one or two Matrons and Fatima Al-Hakim's father, who went everywhere with her. Shannon found a seat near the back and sat quietly. Two seats up, Monica Chavez and Ellen Rodriguez chatted away in Spanish.

It was nearly noon and the sky was clear. With a hydraulic hiss the bus came to a stop before a traffic light, jerked and started up again. Shannon tapped at the armrest to her seat. The driver glanced at his side mirror, waited for a car to pass, turned. Tanya glanced over at Shannon, smiled.

And then they pulled into the lot and pulled to a stop. One of the security men rose and turned on the PA system.

"All right, ladies, I want an orderly group and I want you to stay close. We have some extra policemen here and a guard for each of you. We can't stay long because once word gets out that you're here we may have to deal with fans. All right?"

Mumblings of assent. Girls rose and guards rose with them. The doors popped open. Shannon waited, stood. Her heart was pounding and she wasn't quite sure why.

"Miss O'hea?"

A guard. Tall, stocky. Short black hair and eyes hidden behind sunglasses. She nodded, stepped with him off the bus.

There was a crowd already, moving about. It was unusually warm that day and many wore shorts despite the autumn. Under a half-dome a small band played and a woman sang. As a group the girls stepped towards it. The security men scanned around them and did threat assessments.

Father and son. Father: Approximate age of thirty-eight. African-American. Unarmed. Right-handed. Has shown no notice of subjects.

Son: Approximate age of seven. African-American. Unarmed. Right-handed. Has seen but not recognized subjects.

Time to neutralize: Three seconds each.

Low danger.

Ahead were a row of parked cars.

Automobiles: One Saturn (red), two Honda (blue and silver), one Ford (blue). All unoccupied. One of the Hondas has a low rear tire.

Low danger.

Single male. Slightly intoxicated. Unarmed. Has noticed subjects but has not displayed clear recognition.

Time to neutralize: One second.

Medium danger.

They passed the parked cars and reached the grass. The crowd thickened. Shannon moved with them and she too watched carefully.

Who stands for me? she thought again.

She glanced at her guard.

No.

She looked beyond. A group of kids were moving to the music. Nearby a family had assembled a picnic.

They approached the half-dome. The chief of security glanced at his watch, said something into his radio, turned to them.

"The symphony is up next. I think we have time for a few pieces. Let's have a seat."

One by one they did. The crowd was thickening, old and young, and the guards scanned them all.

A woman approached Tanya, smiling as she did.

The guards moved forward.

Medium danger. Target recognizes subjects.

The woman's partner stepped forward as well.

Approximate ages: Thirty-two (woman) and thirty-five (man). Both Caucasian. Unarmed.

Time to neutralize: Three seconds.

Medium danger, moving to high.

"Are you Tanya Kirilova?" the woman asked.

The guards paused with hands on tear gas spray.

"Yes," Tanya said in her accented English.

The woman's partner moved again and found his way blocked by one of the guards.

"I'm sorry, sir. No closer."

The man's eyes narrowed. The security man did not move.

They watched one another.

Then the man turned to the woman. "Come on," he said. "This guy's an asshole."

The guards turned back to their charges, made a quick count, then another.

The chief raised his radio and snapped a quick order.

Georgie turned at the sound of the siren. Jim turned too. They had moved away from the half-dome as the orchestra stepped onstage and now were deciding on what they should get to drink.

"What's that?"

"Maybe someone got shot."

Jim shook his head. "Too many cops." He stood on tiptoe. "Looks like it's coming from the lot."

"Let's scope it."

"What about Adam?"

"He'll find us. Let's go."

They moved through the growing crowd. Somewhere nearby a baby cried. Jim paused and tried to stand on tiptoe again; Georgie pressed ahead. The crowd broke suddenly.

"What is it?" Jim called.

Georgie froze in place. He was on the lot now, beside a car, and as he took a breath to answer a police cruiser appeared in front of him and he stepped back.

"Shit!" he cried. "Holy fucking shit!"

And there it was.

The bus, windows tinted. The line of dark, serious men. And between them the faces he knew.

Tanya Kirilova, Fatima Al-Hakim, Ellen Rodriguez.

"Shit!" he repeated.

And then there was a policeman in his way, and more policemen everywhere, and the last person climbed up on the bus and the doors closed and it began to move away. The policeman before him spoke.

"All right, son, excitement's over. Back up."

"That was them!"

"I know. Back up."

Georgie did. Someone grabbed his arm. He thrashed, turned.

Jim.

"What, man? What?"

Georgie pointed back at the bus, pulling out of the lot. "Them, dude! I saw them! The cop said it was them! I saw Tanya!"

Jim's eyes went wide. "Shit."

"Yeah."

More cars appeared, blocking the lot. Men emerged from them, and scanners too, sweeping. Policemen began moving through the crowd, looking here, looking there.

"Something's going on," Georgie said.

Jim nodded. "Come on. Let's find Adam."

They started to make their way back to the hot dog cart. A man in black, sinister behind his sunglasses, cut them off without a word.

"That ain't no cop," Jim said.

"No."

They reached the cart and a moment passed. Another policeman passed them. The vendor gave him a smile but was ignored. And then Adam was there.

He wore a look of wonder. Georgie stepped forward.

"What's going on, dude?"

Adam replied in a whisper.

"Shannon. She's gone."

No one. That was who. No one at all. No one save for her, she herself, Shannon O'hea. No one stood for her.

Because no one could. No one knew. No one had been where she was, who she was, what she was. And almost no one cared, either, what she might want, what she might need. Alicia cared but Alicia was young, afraid and new to this. Mother loved but she had no idea what it was to be Shannon, to be watched, monitored, recorded, to have your clothes and hair picked by someone else, to be unable to even walk down the street without having someone there to control you.

No one.

She was far from the park now, lost among the skyscrapers of the city; the Sears Tower, the business district. Busy, active. People moving back and forth, lost in themselves, ignoring her.

Yes!

It was a feeling she had never had before. Out alone, unseen, unwatched. Mundane. Just a girl walking, the wind against her face. She had on a pair of dark glasses and a scarf she had secreted in her purse back at the hotel and she kept her head straight as she walked.

She wanted to dance, to really dance, to spin and cry out. This was the world; this was real. These were people and they were just like her. On impulse, she did a pirouette and threw back her head.

"Oh God," she whispered. "Thank you."

It had been frightening at first. Slipping away as attention focused on Tanya, wondering if the guards had seen her. Losing herself in the crowd and moving quickly, knowing they would not give her much time. And the sirens then, and running, through the pedestrian tunnel beneath Lake Shore Drive, faster and faster with the new freedom of every step, and the fear fading as she reached the other side and slipped into the lobby of a building. Watching as the first police cars arrived, finding her way out the other side and crossing another street to safety.

Here.

She walked, up and over a pedestrian bridge. People moved with her and they moved on when she stopped at the center of the bridge, when she stared out at the park, at the police cars still there. She spoke then, to herself and the world.

"I stand for me."

Georgie reached out and grabbed his friend by the collar.

"What do you mean, man?"

Adam grabbed back. "Be cool! I heard them, dude! It's Shannon!"

"Where?"

"They don't know! But she's here, man! Somewhere!"

Georgie let him go, glanced quickly around.

"They had a bunch of them, man. They came for the concert. There was trouble and they lost her. I saw them bustin' the guy who gave them shit."

Jim moved up. "Holy fuck…She might be here."

Adam nodded. But Georgie was thinking and shaking his head. "No," he said. "Look at how they're scoping this place. If she was here, they'd have found her."

"So where is she?"

Georgie looked around. "Lake or the city. That's it."

"Lake's not fuckin' likely."

"No. The city."

"Let's go."

They walked quickly, afraid that to run would attract attention. Over to the tunnels. The cops were here too, moving through ahead of them.

"Oh shit," whispered Jim.

"Just look cool," Georgie answered. There was a new feeling in him as they moved through the tunnel, as they passed the policemen on the other side and as they produced their IDs for them. It had begun as adrenaline but grew now, grew to more than just a feeling but a confidence as well.

A confidence. But of what? Why would Shannon disappear?

Never mind. You can find her.

Why?

She's Shannon.

No. Not enough.

He led the way; forward, direct, eyes scanning for anything, for that shot of blonde hair, for that face. Ears listening, open for her voice. And as he moved and Jim and Adam moved with him a new thing began to occur to Georgie, a new feeling.

What if she needs my help?

Then you must help her.

Of course. She's Shannon.

No. Not because she's Shannon. Because she's a person and you owe your help to any person, regardless. That's the way it is.

Your way.

He stopped, looked back at his friends. Jim watched him while Adam gazed ahead of them.

"Cool," Jim said. "Too cool."

"Yeah," Georgie said. "Right."

He turned and stepped forward.

You could stay, wander. Look around. But they're looking for you too, even now. They want you and they will have you.

Turn here. That way. Any way.

Any way that does not lead home.

Home.

Cameras, microphones, questions. What's your strategy, Shannon? How would you rate your chances? You're beautiful, Shannon. I love you, Shannon.

Turn for me.

Love for me.

Shannon!

She stopped, paused for a moment and pulled back her scarf, ran fingers through her hair, scratched at her scalp. And the word and the name that it was ran again and again through her head.

Shannon Shannon Shannon Shannon…

"No! Stop it!"

The whisper did. Only the city sounds came now. She drew the scarf back up and looked around, pushed her hands into the pockets of her jeans and stepped forward again.

You could stop, she told herself. Quit. Retire. Get on the next magtrain to Tucson and put all this behind you.

Forget…

And what will they say then? Who will you be? Shannon O'hea, the girl who couldn't handle it?

Fine. Let them say it.

And what will you do?

I don't know. I don't know.

What are you?

I don't know.

She stopped again, reached out a hand and felt the wall of a building. It was brick, solid, and as she felt it things began to clear, just a bit.

You don't know. But they do.

She wandered north, towards an L terminal she had passed early on. A part of her wanted to buy a ticket and ride the train back to the hotel, but a part of her had heard about the dangers of the big city and this part of her was afraid.

The terminal appeared and she went inside, stepped into the public restroom to relieve herself. Even this seemed new and she took a moment to read some of the graffiti scrawled in there.

Who would write these things? Why?

Even freedom brought her no answers.

She stepped outside finally, walked over to the ticket booth. The man behind the glass barely looked up.

"Excuse me," she said.

"Yeah?"

"Is there a phone I can use?"

His voice took on a tone of irritation. "Pay phone right over there."

She went, raised the receiver, pulled out a dollar from her purse and fed it into the machine. There was a click, and she began to dial.

"Claremont Downtown. May I help you?"

They came then, in a hurry. A limousine, two police cruisers. She sat in the terminal as they burst in, sweeping the area with sensors, running, shouting instructions to one another. A security woman appeared in front of her.

"Miss O'hea?"

"Yes."

The woman gripped her arm, pulled her up. The man behind her had his pistol in his hand.

"Let's move! Get her out!"

Then Shannon was lifted, up into the woman's arms and through the doors, into the limousine and away at high speed.

Only then did the woman take the time to look into her face. The hair was mussed, as though someone had been handling it, and the face and the eyes were blank, saying nothing at all.

Chapter 10

The players gathered and the ranks were made. One: Kirilova. Two: O'hea. Three: Rinehart. Four: Li. On and on, pairing for the first matches of the elimination round. The girls came together in the conference room on the upper floor of the museum and watched as this was done, considered their first opponents.

In the city and across the world, the fans and the analysts and the Matrons did likewise.

Did you?

Of course.

But what else did you consider late that September?

Georgie watched himself. Georgie, for the first time, looked inside for his answers. The change had been coming and growing and building and he had felt this and he had been just a bit excited and a bit afraid about it.

Now it was here.

But what to do about it?

He looked over at his poster of Shannon and she stared back at him. He watched it for a long time, watched the eyes, the way they matched her perfect face, watched her little smile, framed in her shining, platinum hair.

And his heartbeat seemed different and he felt the change there.

"Oh, Shannon," he whispered. "What did they do?"

There had been the reports, of course, the shouted questions by reporters and the police snapping back. On the vids, in the papers this morning, on the lips of everyone everywhere.

What happened? Where is she?

There was a mixup, the officer said. She got separated and contacted us. We picked her up. No problem.

What do you mean mixup?

There was a crowd and she got separated from the group.

Reliable sources say a kidnapping. Any comment, Captain?

There was no kidnapping.

Then where is she?

At the Claremont Downtown, of course.

Why haven't we seen her?

Why should you? She chose to have breakfast in her room.

Were there ransom demands? How much was paid? Did they do anything to her?

Nobody did anything.

Will she still be able to compete?

Compete! Compete!

Georgie closed his eyes and lowered his head into his hands. There was a pain in his chest that wouldn't quite go away, a pain that knotted his stomach and made his mouth dry. It made him want to shout like he never had before, to tell them to leave her alone, that he had been there and that he was a part of this now.

Part of what?

He didn't know. But he was, and other things no longer seemed so important. Only Shannon and he.

And the game too.

Somehow. He sat at lunch with Jim and Adam and listened as they gossiped.

"What if it *was* a kidnapping, dude? We could have been right in it."

"Cool. Wonder if the cops busted the guys."

"They busted that one guy. I saw it."

"Yeah. Lady on the vid said it had to be a kidnapping. Shannon wouldn't just walk away; she'd try to get back to the group."

"Yeah. What do you think, Georgie?"

Georgie looked at his friends. His milk carton was still in his hands and he finished it now, reached for his sandwich.

"I wish people would talk about the first round for a change," he said.

Adam's eyes widened. He looked at Jim, who looked back at Georgie. Georgie spoke again.

"I mean, she's back, right? She's gonna compete, right? So what's the big deal?"

"What if the kidnappers fucked with her or something?" Jim asked.

Georgie tensed, formed his hand into a fist. "This is stupid," he said. "Why would they do that?"

"Keep her from playing. That's what the vid said."

"You believe it?"

"I don't know. Maybe."

"Why don't we scope the Claremont and find out?"

Adam shook his head. "There's gonna be a million cops in there. They'll lock the doors."

"We'll stay outside. We'll just scope; won't hurt anyone."

"You're sure?" Jim asked.

"Stay here if you want."

Jim shook his head slowly. "No," he said. "I'll go."

Georgie got home late and Mom and Dad were there and they gave him a lecture about being out. He said nothing as they did and later retired to his room to reflect. He had been right, of course; the hotel had other business and they couldn't close off the area out front. The three of them had wandered around, scoped the cars that pulled up, scoped the entrance to the restaurant and the big entrance to the reception desk and the doors leading back into the maintenance hall. A cop had come up then and had told them to leave, but that was all right because they had seen everything they wanted to anyway. And all the way home Georgie had sat quietly as Adam and Jim kept repeating how cool it was to have gotten this close.

Too cool.

Magnum cool.

But not enough anymore.

Georgie looked at his poster again. Not enough anymore, just looking, just wanting and wondering and fantasizing. He turned on his computer and brought up the sports page, paged through to the evening edition. The eliminations began in four days and there ought to be something about Shannon.

There was. Do you remember?

Shannon had emerged for dinner. Reporters fought to get to her. Cameras rolled and microphones stabbed at her mouth.

"Shannon! Shannon! What happened? Can you tell us?"

Do you remember how she turned away?

Do you remember how they pushed forward again?

"Tell us, Shannon! What did they do to you?"

Her face bumped a mike. She stopped. She turned.
"No comment."
No comment?
No comment?
How dare she!

She sat then, for dinner. Alicia was beside her, and Fatima, and they chatted a bit but the vid didn't pick it up.

And then the dinner report was over and someone was doing predictions.

Georgie switched off the terminal and pulled a notebook from his drawer. It was an impulsive act, sudden and quick and somehow certain.

Because just watching wasn't enough anymore.

He raised a pencil and hesitated.

He had written her before, care of her fan club, a dozen times. Twice he had gotten back a form response, a printed thank you for your support with a false signature. There were stories of boys who got back real letters, really written and signed by her, but these were just stories and he had never met one of these boys.

Not enough. Perhaps that was how he should start. The pencil descended and the first line began its lonely path.

My dear Shannon:

I don't know what is happening to me. I don't know why. But something is calling me to you and I can't stop it. I know you don't know me and you think I'm just another one of the millions who want you, but this is not true. Please understand. Please.

It isn't the game exactly. I'm seeing you different and after you disappeared I tried to find you. Maybe you saw me, in the park. I was with my two friends. They love you too but it's not the same way I do, but like I used to. They want you because you love us in the matrices and I want you that way too but it's something more now with me. I just don't understand how anymore.

I see you alone, Shannon. Are you? I see people using you, like they say the kidnappers did. Please know that if someone was hurting you I would have done anything to stop them. Please know that even if they did hurt you it won't change how I feel for you.

I'll be watching when you play. I can't help it because you are so beautiful, because you make me so happy. But I want you to be happy too,

Shannon. I don't want people to say such mean things about you. When they do please think about me and feel better.

That's all. I know you'll probably never read this but it was important for me to say it. Remember that I'll be thinking about you, Shannon, all the time.

Love, Georgie

He put the pencil down, sat back. He felt better now, as he folded up the letter and stuck it in his desk. He thought back to the hotel entrance, to the reception desk that had just been visible through the large glass doors, and he wondered if there was a letter drop there.

Her first match was in four days.

Perhaps he would try the day after.

Chapter 11

▼

Heard enough? You think that's all? You are thinking perhaps what the billions of others thought, that this was only a sport, that it was harmless and that for many of these girls it was their only chance against a hostile world? Or that Shannon was not so unusual, really, that she was growing up and that girls who are growing up always rebel? Well, that's fine. You can think that, and you can wonder what this is all about, if you like.

It's all in the histories, after all.

But the histories are wrong. Not in what they say but in what they don't.

Don't believe me?

Let's look further. Let's look at another champion.

Remember Neriah York? What do the histories say about her? No, not when she played, but later. What happened to her when puberty had come and gone, when the little champion became a woman?

You shrug. Relax, then, and I'll tell you.

Are you old enough to remember Neriah in her prime? The star girl? She danced the matrices like no one ever had before. To join her in your VR chair was to make love to an angel, to drink stardust and innocence, to speed your thoughts to twice the speed of light. You remember the five world championships? The names are fixed forever: New York, Madrid, Kampala, Auckland, and Beijing. Even what we know now cannot make that fade.

Remember?

She deserved them, those championships, and the immortality that came with them. She deserved it all, and more, perhaps, because soon enough it was gone.

Oh, yes. The tired veteran deserved a rest.

And now the little girls that were today's champions were on their way to see her. Now the children who had grown up worshipping her and her memory, her and the five immortal names, were boarding a flight at O'hare, settling into seats for the short flight north.

Because Neriah had retired to a vast estate just outside her native Toronto and it was close enough for a photo op. The old saluting the new and all that.

Old? Neriah was barely thirty-three.

A bit over twice the age of Shannon O'hea.

A bit over twice the age of the girl who was daring to challenge her legend.

No one really thought of that.

The girls sat on the plane in their perfect, pretty dresses, their Matrons beside them. A few of the girls fidgeted and a few of the Matrons did too.

Shannon did not, and the photographers saw this. They took their pictures, and dictated quiet notes about the composure of the young champion. Alicia stared out the airplane window, out at the wing and the afternoon sky. There is a picture of her, snapped by a photographer who couldn't get quite the angle he wanted on Shannon herself and who settled on the bronze medalist.

Look at it sometime.

It is an interesting study. It really made the papers later, and you don't have to dig very deep to find it. Alicia sits in repose, her little chin supported by her little hand, cupped. There is a shadow over her eyes but the vid was just able to capture a hint of the whites, a hint of the pupils.

A hint, maybe, of what lay below.

Was Alicia afraid, even then?

Toronto and down. Through and out of the busy city, surrounded by the photographers and the reporters and the mayor and two Canadian ministers. Oh, busy, busy! The scenic route, of course. Comfortable limousines for little bodies tired from the uncomfortable first class aircraft seats.

Interview for the local vid station.

How do you like Toronto, Miss O'hea?

It's lovely. Merci beaucoup.

Ah. Français pour les Québécois. Merci, Mademoiselle O'hea. Welcome to Canada.

Even the Mayor looks good beside her.

So they said, and behind the cameras the director and the producer worked their magic to make it all seem spontaneous.

But you want to hear about Neriah, don't you? You haven't forgotten? Very good. Enough of Toronto. They went now, after the formalities. Limos and Matrons and girls. Out of the city and through the country, over roads that got smaller and thinner and rougher, with the press always behind in Chevrolets and Fords and Hondas.

Out to the quiet house of the legend.

And in the cars the Matrons and the reporters whispered the sacred, holy sequence of names.

New York, Madrid, Kampala, Auckland, and Beijing.

But for Shannon, who sat very still, who paid no attention to her Matron as the woman did a quick touch-up on her makeup, there were other words, other sacred things.

Sydney, Cairo, and Moscow.

In the privacy of the limo Shannon let her impassive face fall and she fought for a moment between envy and pride.

"Shannon?" asked her Matron. "Shannon?" And the Matron extended a lipstick, but Shannon only turned away and stared out at the passing road. It was empty out there but in the distance there were lights; homes, these, mundane homes of mundane people. And there was a thirst in Shannon suddenly, rising now and more than a fantasy or an adventure, more than a few short hours as there had been in Chicago. Home, she thought, home. Someplace away, where she would rise with the sun and give her life to the land, to the dark, rich earth and the things it grew.

She stared down at her hands. Rough from work that you could feel, that you could hold. Yes. A life there, real and solid, like Chicago had been but more, where she would never have heard of Shannon O'hea, would never have seen herself in a white leotard in a VR chair.

What would it be like, to be like that?

Neriah now. She was a mother. Twin boys and a little girl. She was a wife also, and her husband was ten years her senior. He was not there that evening because he could not stand to watch what he knew would happen. Oh, he had tried to call off the visit, had tried hard to convince Neriah that it would be a strain on her. When that failed he brought up the children and the strain on them.

When that failed too he left and got a hotel room in Toronto, where like an addict he could not help but watch anyway from the VR chair in his room.

But at least he wasn't there.

Neriah met the Matrons like a queen in her court. They bowed in deference and watched her cold, blue eyes. They got out of the way when she moved past them and faced the line of girls who had succeeded her. And no one said anything until she did.

"Welcome. We have dinner for you." She extended her graceful arm and indicated the dining room. At that moment Monica Chavez stepped forward with a little bouquet and spoke in her native tongue:

"Gracias, Señora."

In his VR chair far away, Neriah's husband tensed.

But the hostess only smiled and took the gift, held it and stared with her rigid smile as the rest of the children filed by, each greeting her in their own tongue, each saying the same thing, rehearsed on the plane.

Oh? You disagree? You say Neriah's smile vanished as Shannon faced her?

Of course it did.

New York, Madrid, Kampala, Auckland, and Beijing.

Sydney, Cairo, and Moscow.

Don't be surprised. Life is like that. Nobody likes being eclipsed, especially when bits of their brain are burned out.

And that's what you didn't know. It's true; think about it. A competitor like Neriah never leaves the ring voluntarily; the sport is no less a drug than heroin for them. It's a high, and when they're high they forget that there's a low. This was Neriah's secret, the thing they kept quiet, the thing they had hushed up after her last match, after that amazing performance when, just for a moment, she had made Intersect transcend itself, become more than we ever thought it could be.

More than joy but something else, just for a few seconds.

Neriah looked fine, of course. She was still young, and quite beautiful, her hips now swelled from womanhood and childbearing, and her bosom still firm beneath her emerald-green evening gown. But her final year in Intersect had cost her much. Where she once danced like an angel she found one day that she could no more; her love was gone, you see. Her love, her compassion, her inner beauty. Burned out selectively because that's what she had used to secure herself as a legend in the matrices.

And just when she had touched something new.

I know. I know. It wasn't fair, but it happened. There had always been those who protested the sport, but there was such a joy in it, a joy for the billions in their VR chairs, that the shattered lives of a minority of players were deemed inconsequential, were brushed off as accidents.

Accidents. Little girls who became women who were not quite whole. Did you care, then? Did I? No. We are all, in our own little ways, guilty.

Guilty just as Neriah was with her own children, raised without the love she had once shared with the world.

Was that why her smile vanished when she met Shannon O'hea? Was it not envy, but pity?

Perhaps. But what she showed was clear.

Hate. Raw, pure hate that shook the young champion to the bone.

"Thank you, Madame," Shannon managed. She curtsied then, a gentle, perfect motion, legs crossed and fingers pinching the hem of her dress as she extended it.

That's when Neriah's husband began to shout, and to kick, because as you know a man in a VR chair feels just like he's right at the point of transmission.

"Leave her alone, you bitch! Don't you dare!"

< STRESS LIMITS EXCEEDED.

< CONTACT BROKEN.

< PLEASE EXIT THE VR CHAIR.

< THANK YOU.

Neriah was rich, anyway, and could afford to pay for the broken furniture.

They sat Shannon and Alicia together because the photographers had requested it. To Shannon's left was Cain, who was the eldest of Neriah's twins and whose face was a hard slab of marble and whose little suit pinched tightly at the collar. But he was handsome in a pretty, juvenile sort of way and the producer had thought to ask a subtle "what if" by placing him and Shannon together.

Publicity matchmaking. Who knows? If they had a romance when they were older these vids would be worth an obscene chunk of money and probably a promotion.

And they looked good together, anyway.

To Alicia's right was Tanya, and then Monica Chavez, and then little Susie York, whose only mercy in life was that Neriah forbade any involvement for her daughter in gaming. Li Yon, then, who ate with chopsticks because the producer and the director insisted, and finally Neriah herself.

A black widow in her lair, someone said, much, much later. Were these her children or her prey?

Cain pulled at his collar, looked uncomfortably across at Li Yon. She ate quietly with the unfamiliar chopsticks. Servants brought a second course and Neriah

looked over at Alicia and then at Shannon. The floor director snapped a quick order to a technician.

"Get that camera off her. Shit! Did that get out?"

"No sir."

"Well, thank God. Give me a close-up on the Mexican Chavez."

They ate. You've seen it. Lots of camera time on Shannon and Cain, the poor boy. You've seen how they brought out the pudding by twos and somehow managed to set the two cups so very close; you've seen how they made him sit beside her on the couch later despite the misery in his eyes. She tried to make him comfortable, tried holding his hand and whispering soft reassurances to him, but it did no good. Finally, out of mercy, she thanked him formally for his company and moved away.

And the producer and the director each used language that was really not appropriate for little girls to hear.

Neriah moved among the children with the grace of a gymnast. She spoke with each of them, told little stories about her own years in the game, told of her championships and the long years it took to reach them. She smiled her false smile and gave them each a false courtesy and wondered when there was only Shannon O'hea left if perhaps her despicable husband hadn't been right after all.

From behind one of the cameras the director was waving her in Shannon's direction.

Little bitch. So pretty in pink. Little bow in her hair. Little white legs in little white stockings.

They say you're good, little bitch. I wonder just how good that is?

Neriah stepped toward Shannon O'hea.

New York, Madrid, Kampala, Auckland, and Beijing.

Shannon looked up from where she sat.

Sydney, Cairo, and Moscow.

And Neriah smiled her best smile at the little champion.

"Come," she said. "I'd like to talk."

They went away, the two of them. Away from the vids and the others and the world. In desperation, the producer romanticized the whole thing. Something secret among the past and future champions. A symbolic passing of greatness. Yes, it was romance and nothing more. You don't think they lie on the vids?

All the time, my friend.

But you cannot know this because only Shannon O'hea and Neriah York were there. There, in the quiet trophy room where not even Neriah's husband dared tread. A place dusty with past glory.

"Sit," Neriah told Shannon, and Shannon did.

Neriah went to the first trophy, the first championship. She took the accompanying medal and laid it over her slender neck, against the emerald-green evening gown.

New York.

"You keep your medals, Miss O'hea?"

"Yes."

Neriah turned. The medal seemed small on her, resting against her breast. Small because it was designed for a little girl to wear.

"Why, Miss O'hea?"

Shannon said nothing.

"Do you know what these medals are, Miss O'hea? These little championships?" Neriah paused and stroked the gold pendant as though it was something sexual. "They're what you did, not what you do. People forget them, soon enough."

Shannon rose, stepped back from the chair. There was no mask on Neriah's face now, no excuse for one. Neriah advanced, reached for another medal and extended it to the girl.

Madrid.

"Put it on, little one."

Shannon shook her head, glanced at the door.

Neriah's hand shot out, closed on her shoulder, crushed the soft material of Shannon's dress against Shannon's skin.

"Wear it!" Neriah hissed. "You've worn them before, haven't you?"

"Please...It isn't right. It's yours."

"And I'm telling you to put it on."

Neriah pushed the medal forward, looped the silken band around Shannon's neck, pulled the girl close with it.

"Yes," she whispered, her voice a ragged hiss. "I won that, Miss O'hea. I beat the best in the world for that. If you had been there I would have beaten you too. Do you understand?"

Shannon had become rigid with fear. She nodded, her little hands on Neriah's adult ones.

"No you don't. You have no idea." Neriah's grip tightened. "Listen! Do you know how I won it?"

This Shannon could not answer. She shook her head. Neriah's voice did not change.

"I won it the way you win yours. I won it by loving the world. I danced in the matrices and they loved me back, begged me for more." Neriah's face twisted with growing rage. "And I gave and I gave, O'hea. Like you give. Like a little whore. You are a little whore, aren't you?"

At last the first tear escaped Shannon's eye, rolled down her cheek. And the truth rose in terror: this was no game, no veneer of truth to be manipulated by reporters and commentators until it tasted good and you began to believe it despite what you had seen. This was herself and Neriah, alone and true. And Shannon was afraid.

"Aren't you?" Neriah growled. "Aren't you a whore? I was. I am. My children are a whore's children. My husband is a whoremonger."

She began to tighten the silken band, tight around Shannon's neck, tighter and tighter, until Shannon cried out.

"No!"

"Yes!"

Shannon screamed as the noose began cutting off her air, and she kicked and struggled for a moment until Neriah pulled her close.

"You are living a lie," Neriah whispered.

"No!"

Cold hate. Raw, brutal in the words. "Listen, Shannon O'hea. I've seen you in the matrices, and you're good. There is a way to show more, to let them see what they have done. I found it and so can you."

No words; only terror.

"The higher brain is nothing. It's a game. It isn't real. You know it and they know it." Neriah's nostrils flared and her hands quivered with her hate. "Go to the base, O'hea. The lower brain. Go to what they *really* are, all of them. Everything is in there. Use it on them."

Neriah let go, and Shannon dropped to the floor, gasping. She fought the medal loose and looked up, her vision blurred by tears. Neriah was staring at her and Shannon did not move.

She watched instead.

She watched as Neriah paced to the cabinet and Auckland sailed across the room to crash against the fine mahogany wall. She heard as the woman screamed and slapped Beijing to the floor.

"I hate you!" Neriah screamed. "I hate you I hate you! I hate all of you! I gave you everything! I want it back! Do you hear me?"

Kampala then, in her hands. Pulling on the strap, scratching at the smooth metal, screaming.

"Give it back! Give it back! You never said I had to give it up!"

And Kampala flew, out and away, impacting the wall behind Shannon with a heavy thunk.

Neriah turned, took the door to the cabinet, brought her own head against it hard. A crack formed in the glass pane, which shattered as she hit it again. She slipped then, stunned, and slid to the floor. Blood ran down her face and into her eyes as she brought up her knees and began to rock slowly.

"I want to love again," she whispered.

A moment passed. Shannon pulled herself up until she was squatting.

"Please," she said. "I don't understand."

Neriah looked at her, eyes wide beneath the blood.

"Lower brain," she said. "Find the way and use it. Make them pay. You're good enough, Miss Shannon O'hea. Make them stop."

Shannon said nothing, only rose to her feet and backed away.

Chapter 12

Mysteries draw crowds. The bigger the better, and it is an odd thing that the truth behind a mystery is often not nearly as interesting as the fact of the mystery itself. Oftentimes too, the speculation takes on a life of its own and becomes its own truth and the real truth is turned into a lie by popular demand.

Remember, after Toronto? What were you thinking then? Were you like the billions of others, watching like you never had before?

Watching, because suddenly our princess was a mystery?

What did Neriah say to Shannon? Why did only Shannon return?

It's not fair, giving advice to only one girl. She should tell us all.

Shannon! Shannon! What did she say?

No answer, just as after the episode in the park.

No answer.

The mystery grew.

And Georgie was not so typical anymore.

He watched the vids now, all the time. He saw the mystery and he wondered too, about Neriah, about the park. But Georgie saw something we did not, as we were glued to the words of our sportscasters, as we anticipated what Shannon would say when someone shoved a microphone into her face.

He saw us, and what we were.

Oh, Shannon, it's not fair…

Leave her alone!

I love her!

He saw what we were doing. You and I, lost in our new truths, our created truths, lost in the things we wanted to believe.

Georgie had his letter, tucked safely away inside an envelope in his backpack. He was going to deliver it, drop it with her name on it in the hotel maildrop, bet against the odds that someone would find it and figure it was meant for her but that it had been misplaced. They would take it to her, slip it under her door or hand it to her, and she would read it and know how he felt.

Days passed, though, and it stayed in his pack.

In truth he was afraid, and when he did get downtown it was always with Jim or Adam and he didn't want them knowing about his plan. They were not rivals, not really, because he knew he could dominate them now, but this was a personal thing and besides, they were beginning to say nasty things about Shannon just like the people on the vids.

Adam, at lunch: "I don't know what her problem is. Matches start tomorrow and she just stays up in her room and doesn't say anything."

Jim: "Maybe she's just getting ready."

"But we got a right to know. That's what my dad says. That's what they said on the news."

Georgie spoke slowly. "Why? Why do we got a right?"

Adam watched him. "Because that's the way it is. That's the game, dude."

Jim nodded. Georgie looked back at his food. A slice of pizza, broccoli, carrots, a breadroll. It didn't have much taste, not today, and his hand went to the surface of his backpack and stroked the material over the secret place with his letter.

"That doesn't seem fair," he said.

"Fair? For what they pay her? For that money I'd shit my pants right on camera! We got a right!"

Georgie shook his head. Adam grabbed his arm.

"What's the matter with you, dude? Don't you want to know what she's doing?"

Georgie shuddered. Yes, in fact, he did. Absolutely. He wanted to know everything about her, everything public and private, intimate and mundane. He wanted to know her thoughts and he wanted to know how she sat in the VR chamber before a match, whether she dressed sock-shoe sock-shoe or sock-sock shoe-shoe. Everything they asked about her he wanted answered too.

What was so different about him, then?

Jim was speaking but Georgie didn't hear him. Adam answered but his words made no difference.

And Georgie rose, pulled on his pack, mumbled an excuse and walked away.

Home. No scoping that afternoon. Just the vid, in the living room. He pulled his knees up and stared at the screen as the latest predictions came on.

First round. Any thoughts, Jeff?

I like the matchup between Al-Hakim and Wendy Kaye of Australia. Kaye's been a real surprise in the prelims; quite a fighter. And watch Kirilova and Schultz; ought to be a good one.

Good. Let's turn to the Americans.

No surprises there. Alicia's a shoe-in; Rodriguez ought to be fine.

What about O'hea?

You got me, Brad. No figuring with her anymore.

All right, Jeff. Thanks. As you know, our own Susan Jacobs had a chance to talk with Tanya Kirilova this morning. Tanya's the top seed and she had some interesting things to say. Lets go to that interview now...

They did. Georgie hit the mute and closed his eyes. What was this feeling? What did it mean? His Shannon was in danger somehow but there was nothing he could do about it. And what danger? How? How could he warn her if he didn't understand it himself?

A hand, then, on his shoulder. He started.

"Georgie?"

Mom. He opened his eyes, looked up.

"I'm sorry, dear. I didn't mean to frighten you."

He shook his head. "No. That's okay."

She moved around the couch, sat. "Are you feeling all right?" she asked.

"Fine."

"More sportsvids?"

He rubbed at his brow, nodded. "Yeah."

"I see." She paused. "I got a call today, from your history teacher. She said you haven't been paying much attention in class."

"No. I have."

"Georgie, she said your grades have been slipping."

"She just doesn't like me."

His mother said nothing, only looked over at the pictures on the silent vid. Her hands touched one another, gripped, released. Her face was tight and he could just smell her, a mix of perfumed antiperspirant and old mouthwash. She looked back at him.

"It's the game, isn't it?" she said.

He looked over at her, shrugged.

"Shannon O'hea." Mom sighed, reached for the remote and turned off the vid completely. "Shannon O'hea." She reached over and took his hand. "Georgie, watching a few matches is fine, but you can't let it control you."

"It doesn't," he said.

"Georgie—"

"It doesn't, I tell you!"

Her face grew firm. "All right, then. Let's prove it. No more vid until Shannon's first match. Stick with your homework, Georgie, until then. If you do, you can watch the match. If you can't..." She shook her head.

"That's not fair."

"It's what I say you're going to do. That's three days, Georgie. You come straight home from school and you do your homework and you can watch the match. I mean it. Do you understand?"

He shook his head, looked down. She didn't understand and he didn't know how to tell her so she would. "It's not fair," he said. "I have to—"

Her grip on his hand tightened. "Do this," she said, "Or there's no more Intersect. Period."

Now Georgie nodded slowly.

The three days passed as eons.

Jim and Adam scoped the museum and the hotel every afternoon while Georgie went straight home. He heard little things at lunch, little bits of information that kept him going.

Shannon was at dinner last night. She didn't say anything.

How did she look? How did she seem?

She's Shannon, dude. She looked great.

But she didn't talk much. Reporters were pissed about that.

Did she smile? Where did she sit?

Next to Alicia. Sure she smiled, some.

Still couldn't watch, huh, Georgie?

Nope. Can't scope, either.

What a down, man. That sucks.

Yeah.

Eons. Seconds as minutes, minutes as hours. And while he sat doing homework, or in class, or pestering Jim and Adam for information, his Shannon was alone, hiding from the Jims and the Adams and the sportscasters and the people who wanted to use her, to pick her apart.

I'm coming, Shannon. Please wait for me.

Please.

Tanya defeated Helga Schultz. Li Yon defeated Anna Solveg. And the world wept with joy, anticipating.

Anticipating the day.

The day that came.

Georgie raced home from school, through the front door. Mom was there, watching the vid. She looked up at him and she smiled.

"Hello, Georgie."

He spoke between breaths.

"Tonight's the night, Mom. First match."

She nodded. "Go do your homework. I'll make sure you don't miss anything."

"Mom—"

"Go on, Georgie."

He did. The hours passed. Dinner. Dad asked him how school was going.

Fine. Fine.

Good, Georgie. Ready for tonight?

Yeah. Oh, yeah.

So am I. Think she'll win?

Oh, Dad…

Seven o'clock. VR chairs sliding from their places in the wall. Settling in, lowering the facials.

Beginning.

Georgie sat back, relaxed. He smiled as the system came on. The volume rose and he saw the sportscasters.

"Well Jeff, this has been an unusual tournament."

"To say the least. And Shannon has been the most unusual of all."

"What do you think Neriah York told her?"

"I don't have any idea. Awfully rude, though, not to come back out at her own party."

"She was always a moody one. I remember the tournament in Beijing."

"Who can forget it?"

"You think it had anything to do with the kidnapping?"

"Well, Brad, who knows? Did Neriah ever disappear like that?"

"I don't think so. And they still say it wasn't a kidnapping."

"They say. You ask me, Brad, they lie a lot. You know what Shannon O'hea's worth to this country?"

"Money or pride? I say they give those girls too much freedom."

"I agree. Too much."

"Let's see what she can do today. What odds do you give Pickett?"

"Long, ha ha. Unless something happened to Shannon while she was gone."

"We'll see, won't we?"

They faded, the knowing smiles still on their handsome faces. Georgie inhaled and held the breath as he waited for his queen to come.

And she did.

Shannon, electric. Oh yes. Shannon perfect symmetry, perfect mathematics and logic and in that a perfect love. She spread wings before him, before the world. There was a girl beside her too, a faded idea of a girl, someone unknown and unimportant who would dare to challenge her beauty.

"Shannon..." he whispered, and she turned to him and smiled. His head fell back and the first tears came.

She and the other took up positions, faced off. The other began, jumping for the advantage, sending a stream of perfect light across, meant to shear his Shannon in half.

But Shannon was gone and there again.

Gone and there again. Gone and there.

And she was true, and she was pure, and he could feel the power of her, surging through him.

Because Shannon was growing. Georgie moaned, cried out, as her soul touched his. Reaching with the bare essence of her beauty, pulling theorems and gigabytes from deep recesses far away, taking him along as she rode the links across continents, around and around the world.

Oh dear God dear God dear God...

The other girl struck back but it was like she wasn't there at all.

Around, around. Spinning. Flecks of being, of herself, settled in his eyes and mixed with tears, ran down his cheeks with them. And before him her smile, her kind, loving face, lips just pursed in perfect harmony, a song of angels floating from between them.

"Shannon..." he begged. "Please..."

Please. Please.

Remember?

We all felt it, that day. Because suddenly there was more to her, something we had never felt before. More than love but a joy, a pure, gentle, simple thing. Something new and something powerful that drew on other emotions, other feelings.

And the match ended then because the poor other girl could not defend against this.

No one could.

Chapter 13

▼

There is a way, but how? And what? And why?

What had it meant?

Shannon sat in her room, staring at the wall, hands crossed in her lap. On the table by the door there was a tray with her lunch, eaten now; behind her was the screen of the vid, blank now, silent.

There was no need to turn it on because she knew what they were saying on it. About her.

Always. Days had passed and she had advanced again. The field was narrowing, the strong pushing the weak aside, now watching each other, planning the next match. The big names: Kirilova, O'hea, Rinehart, Li. Those with the potential to upset: Al-Hakim, Chavez of Mexico and Chavez of Brazil and Armeneau.

Names on screens behind oddsmakers. Just names.

Strangers she knew better than her own brother.

Shannon stood, walked to the window. It was cloudy over the lake, misty and gray. Cold tones that matched what she was feeling. She had memorized the view by now, the lake, the skyscrapers, the street below and the parkland beside it. Now as she stared she wrapped her arms tightly across her chest and shivered.

What is this?

Nothing. That was really it, wasn't it? No feeling, anywhere, but deep down, sensing that feelings are there, terrible, powerful feelings that you don't quite understand. She ran her right hand over her left shoulder, felt the soft texture of her blouse, the small joint underneath. No match for the strength of an adult.

The bruises were fading but still visible, if you looked.

Neriah had touched her there, had gripped her, pulling her close to the fierce hatred in her eyes. And Neriah had choked her, had said things to her that no one else ever had.

Terrible things.

But there had been more too. More words.

You're good enough, Shannon O'hea.

Good enough for what?

To do what?

Shannon rubbed at her neck, at the soft skin. And she whimpered softly and turned from the window. The strap from the medal had not left a mark on her neck and she had told no one what had happened. She had meant to, at first, as she ran down the hall of Neriah's home, away from the demon who had once so loved the world. But as Shannon ran, as she reached the huge living room, as the other girls and the Matrons and the reporters and the cameramen turned to her, the truth had come to her again.

Only *I* stand for me.

Only I.

And so she had been silent, explaining that Neriah wasn't feeling well and that she had retired for the evening. Nothing more, no matter how hard they asked. Not a word, even though it was all she could do to keep from trembling and crying out.

Then it was back here and up to her room and she had stayed here ever since.

Afraid? Yes.

But what had Neriah meant? That was as important as the fear.

Maybe more.

Mother came in. Shannon turned.

"Hello, dear," the woman said. "Feeling better?"

Shannon nodded. "Some."

"You have a match tomorrow, you know. Are you ready for it?"

"Yeah."

Mother was sharp. She saw. "Honey, is there something wrong?"

"No."

The word had a bitter taste, the sourness of a lie mixed with anger and frustration. I could say, she knew. She could tell Mother if she could tell anyone, but it would mean nothing and it would do nothing and it would solve nothing. Because Mother did not know and could not know what it was like.

To be Shannon O'hea.

But should you try? How long can you keep this up?

"Shannon," Mother said. She moved forward and Shannon felt her arm go around her and guide her to the bed. "You've been doing nothing but stare out that window all day. Something's wrong and I want you to tell me what it is."

Shannon shook her head again.

"What happened in the park, Shannon?"

"Nothing."

"Shannon, you disappeared for an entire afternoon. They found you in an L terminal and they told me you weren't kidnapped. That means you ran away. Why?"

Policemen, security, checks. An interrogation. That had been the cost of her afternoon downtown. The woman doctor and her questions and her tape recorder.

What happened, Shannon? Did someone take you? Did they touch you, down there? Here's a doll; show me.

No. No one took me. I got scared. I got lost.

Why did it take you so long to call? If someone hurt you, we won't tell anyone. We've already told the reporters you just got lost.

I did.

All right. We need to examine you, Shannon, take some blood, check some things.

"Shannon? Can you hear me?"

She spoke slowly. "I had to get away, Mother."

"Away? Why?"

Shannon leaned forward, rested her brow in her hands. "I don't know. But I'm all alone, Mother."

Mother pulled her close, kissed the top of her head. "No, Shannon. I'm here."

She wanted to shake her head, to explain how no, no, this wasn't true, not like she meant. But it occurred to Shannon then that Mother *was* there, had always been there. She answered instead, "Only here. Not out there."

"Shannon, wherever you are, I'm with you. Remember that. You're my little girl."

"I'm just confused."

Mother kissed her again. "No. It just seems that way. Give it time and it'll all be clearer. It's part of growing up."

Shannon looked up, first at her mother, then at the room, the computer, the window, the vid. And when she spoke it wasn't soft anymore.

"No. This is not a part of growing up."

Mother stared and Shannon could feel her gaze. "Shannon..." she began, but Shannon only shook her head and went to her computer and turned it on. Theorems came up, strategies and designs. Shannon sat down and began working.

"Shannon," Mother said, "If you need me..."

A slight nod in answer, nothing more.

Mother left quietly.

There is a way.

No.

Shannon moved from the desk and sat down on the bed again and closed her eyes. She tried to picture things in her head that were not there, things that were not real.

Like me.

What am I?

What do they see when they look at me?

Our angel. Our heroine. America's best hope. Perfect, beautiful. Queen of the matrix.

Is that all?

Yes.

Is that all I am?

Hesitation, truth. No.

I'm a person, too. I have two arms and two legs and a head and a mouth and ears and eyes. Just like you do. And I can be happy sometimes and sad sometimes, just like you are.

Just like everyone, just like anyone.

To stand in the crowd instead of before it. Not to be Shannon O'hea but to be Shannon Smith or something like that. To be Alicia's friend because you live next door or go to the same school, not because no one else can be your friend.

The thought came again. You could quit. Retire.

And then what? What will really change?

Voices, hammering her. Microphones and cameras and demands. Taking as she gave, over and over. Neriah, too, in there, accusing, telling.

Shannon! Say something to us! What happened?

Where did you go?

How can you still be Alicia's friend, after a defeat like that?

You make us so proud.

You make us so happy.

You make us so angry.

So angry. Give us more. More.
There is a way.

And the way was clear and the way was joy.
For us.
This you cannot forget.
For Shannon was perfect in the matrices, those times.
Juanita Gregorio; defeated in five minutes of heaven. Katherine Bent, down in seven. Impossible moves, actions, steps. New things to feel, new emotions. And now the sportscasters were not asking if her disappearance had brought her down, but what had happened to bring her up.
Was it Neriah?
No. Neriah was never like this. She played the same way as everyone else, only better.
Except at the end, in the last matches, when she touched something new. Was that it? Has she given Shannon an unfair edge?
Let's see. Look at the telemetry from Neriah. Are they the same?
Maybe. But their styles are different. Same goal, different road. I've never seen this sort of play before.
Shannon is World Champion. You expect her to be good.
No. This is unbelievable.
Yamada, down in six minutes. And they asked Shannon then, what she had done. They put it on the vids worldwide, broke into news and soaps and dramas, so that we could all hear her answer, her plan, her secret.
Remember? The quiet smile, the eyes, knowing? The words, spoken softly and not repeated?
"Find the way."

Chapter 14

Different. Different. What?

Look! Take stock. What was before, and what is now? That's the difference, the special thing. That's what you want to find.

Or do you?

Georgie looked at Shannon, at her face on the poster, in the books, on the vid. The talk show, sitting by Hugh Bradley, looking out at the crowd.

What does she see? What am I seeing looking at her?

Go back. Before. Before the tournament, before the magtrain terminal. Go back...to Moscow. To Cairo, to Sydney, even to Li Yon's championship in Buenos Aires. Go back and see who you were, Georgie. Go back and remember how you felt.

Joy, love. For the game, for the beautiful girl with the shining hair, for what she gave you in the matrices. Your adolescent love as you turned eleven, then twelve, then thirteen and fourteen and now fifteen. Worshipping what she seemed to be.

Oh, Shannon, what you give to me...

More, Shannon, more.

Back then, not now. What was now?

Different. It was not her that had changed, not at all. She still loved in the matrices; more, in fact, than ever before. She was still the perfect, ideal girl, worshipped and adored just like before, by boys just like him who saw what she showed them. No, it was not her at all, it was him. It was Georgie, new and different, beyond what his friends could see, looking behind the mask that was Shannon O'hea, seeing glimpses of what and who she really was.

Maybe. Who knew?
She was still so far away.

Another afternoon; lunch, classes, the bell at the end of the day. And Georgie, slipping out unseen, away from Jim and Adam, towards the L terminal, south, to downtown. To the lakefront with his pack over his shoulder and his hidden cargo inside.

On his mission to reach her.

Have you ever had a mission, a goal? Have you ever been one of the extraordinary ones who walk at the edge?

You are close, now.

Just by listening.

Georgie stood in the shadow of the great hotel and stared up at the glittering facade of the two towers. He seemed alone then, by himself against the conventions of all the world, facing the impossible odds, facing the scorn and anger and envy of an entire world. Just me, just you, just Georgie, because we dare to answer what most fear so much.

Ourselves.

Georgie stepped forward, crossed the street. He stood silently before the glass doors of the lobby, watched the doorman closely, all suited up in his uniform with his hat and the stripes on his perfectly pressed pants. Georgie waited for a busload of tourists, waited until they were all climbing from the bus, moved forward again.

Then he stepped inside.

There was security here; the lobby to the north tower was guarded, off limits. You could see the guards by the elevators, by the front desk, by the doors to the restaurant. Policemen and the silent men in dark coats, watching, waiting, ready.

The tourists mingled about the lobby to the south tower. Their guide appeared and said something in German, and some of them answered. Georgie watched, looked toward the desk again. There *was* a maildrop there, just a few feet away, but the distance seemed to grow, to stretch, each time he took a breath.

Too far, too far, too many people here.

He stepped away, toward the restrooms. Reporters were clustered outside the door, checking cameras and equipment, talking in low tones about setups for dinner, about angles and broadcast lines. Georgie passed them and entered the men's room, went right to a stall and sat. There was the sudden need to urinate, satisfied quickly, and when he had finished he zipped open his pack and pulled out his letter.

She's going to think I'm an idiot, he thought suddenly.
What if she's what everyone says she is?
What if she's not alone, not afraid?
What if I am?
For five seconds, ten seconds, twenty seconds, the doubts raged. Georgie looked at the envelope, at her name printed there, and for a second more wondered if he had misspelled it. It was sealed now and he thought suddenly that he had put the wrong page inside, that after all his trouble Shannon would wind up with one of his mother's shopping lists.
No, no, stupid. You checked it ten times!
He had to pee again. He did, the letter held between his lips.
All right, listen. You wrote this letter. It says the truth and you know she has to be lonely. She gets it, she can read it or throw it away or laugh at it. Fine. But this is your only chance because soon enough she'll be gone and that'll be that. Just go out, drop it in the box. She either gets it or she doesn't but you've done your part.
All right?
All right.
Now zip up your fly.

He turned, stepped out, slung his pack over his shoulder. Out past the reporters, back toward the main desk. The Germans were still there and the guide was talking to the receptionist. Step, step, step. Towards them, towards the box. Letter in hand, held against your side, so certain that you look suspicious; are they watching you?
Glance around. Look casual now, Georgie, don't give it away. Security by the elevators is watching the tourists. Cop over there is looking at the guide.
All right. One more step, two more steps.
Georgie took them, rested his hand against the mahogany counter, so close. The receptionist noticed but she was busy. Raise the letter. Up, drop it in.
In!
Turn! Go!
He did. One step, two.
And that was all.
The policeman got him on the first try.
"Looking for something, son?"
A hand, on Georgie's arm. A grip, too tight to break. He pulled anyway and looked up.

"Huh?"
"What was that you dropped in the box?"
Georgie shook his head.
"Nothing."
The cop grinned. "Oh? Let's see."
He pulled, and Georgie followed. It was silent now, in the lobby; the Germans were watching and the guide was watching and the receptionist was watching. And in the silence Georgie's cry seemed all the louder.
"No!"
The policeman stopped, pulled him close. "You want to go downtown, boy? Messing with the mail's an offense, and it doesn't matter your age." He pulled again, reached the counter, spoke to the receptionist.
"Let's see it. Ought to be on top."
She reached in, pulled out Georgie's letter. "There," she said. "No stamp. For Shannon O'hea."
Security was there suddenly. Two men; dark glasses, dark coats. The policeman handed them the envelope, turned to Georgie.
"This a bomb, boy? Poison?"
Georgie shook his head wildly. "No! No!"
"We'll get it sniffed," one of the men said, and took it away.
The cop nodded, frisked Georgie quickly and pulled him toward a couch in the middle of the lobby, pushed him down. "Now you wait," he said, and stood there, glaring.
The shaking began, uncontrollable shaking that grew as Georgie tried to fight back the tears. He wanted to explain but words would not come; only the silence of his ragged breathing, his dry mouth, the sudden urge to vomit.
Then the voice of security again, high overhead.
"It's clean. Just another fan."
The cop: "Right. Thanks. We'll send him home."
Security moved away.
The cop again: "You got ID, boy?"
Georgie nodded. "Yeah, yeah."
"Show me...slow."
Georgie produced his wallet. The policeman scrutinized it for a moment, pulled out his mike and spoke.
"This is 1147. I need a car."

Chapter 15

▼

They were times unlike any before. It was the game but it was more. More power, more feeling. A new level of joy that turned men and women into addicts unlike anything they had ever been. Do you remember now? How Shannon remade us, what we were, what we could feel in our VR chairs?

Our numbers grew, we who watched. The record, set by Neriah and Velasquez, was three and a half billion people. Shannon went to three and three quarters, then four, then four and a half. She was no longer America's girl but belonged to the world, to planet Earth. She gave us joy, in those brief days, and because she did there was no longer any reason to seek it ourselves.

Oh, Shannon, love me.

Dance for me, think for me, *be* for me.

How odd that she herself could not feel the joy.

Don't believe me?

Perhaps you have never been worshipped.

Yes. Because that was the very thing we did to her. How would Christ feel, returning to the masses of the imperfect who demand salvation from without, not knowing that it lies within? How must it be, to be seen as perfect, ideal, to be denied the very natural human failures that are our right?

Days passed. Tanya advanced with confidence. Li Yon devastated an upstart Laotian. Fatima edged out Amanda Sawyer. And the world watched these matches but only so much, because Intersect with them was not Intersect with Shannon and that's what we had gotten used to now.

A few words about Shannon, Tanya. Can you beat her?

I don't know. We'll see.
They say she's better than last year. That's a tough challenge.
Yes.
Well, we'll see how you do. Good luck, Tanya.
Thank you.
Pause. We off the air?
Yeah.
Poor kid. Shannon's gonna kill her.

Shannon who stayed out of sight, hidden.
There was more than the world, too, more than the demands. There was Neriah, and dreams. The face, contorted and screaming, and what lay behind it. For behind that face, Shannon knew, there was something important, something Neriah had needed to tell her but that she could not.
Neriah, pulling tightly on the silken strap, choking out the air.
Whispering.
You are living a lie.
Tighter now, tighter.
You're good enough.
Good enough.
Good enough.
There is a way.
And air, suddenly, as Shannon came awake with a cry. Gasping air, drunk in gulps. Her bedsheets, her nightgown, cold in sweat, shivering from the fear and the chill and begging silently to empty air.
"Stop…Please stop…"
And the next day crushing Cathy Nesbitt in three minutes flat.

The mothers watched too. It was not so easy for them, to see Shannon so perfect, because each of them could not help but see their daughters in the game with her, overshadowed, defeated. It was not fair, they said, to have to face such an adversary, not sporting. And that was the point of the game, wasn't it? Competition was what made Intersect so beautiful; if all we wanted was to see Shannon perform we could just set up a stage for her, like the commentator on the vid said we should.
There's an idea. She could perform all the time then.
Here comes her mother now.
I have nothing to say to her.

Mrs. O'hea knew these things, all of them. She heard them all, even the whispers, the rumors. Shannon's Matron was a good source of information and anyone in the legal profession must be able to listen well. Now Mrs. O'hea would sit, alone, in the hotel lounge, while the other mothers kept away, whispering and talking amongst themselves.

Shannon must not know of these jealousies, she thought. It's not fair to pressure her like that.

She's under enough pressure already.

Maybe we'll go see a doctor. She didn't look well this morning.

Thank heavens for Alicia.

This last revelation was a bit startling; Mrs. O'hea had been as concerned as anyone last year in Moscow, but Alicia was a good girl and Shannon certainly needed someone her own age to talk with.

A waiter appeared by her little table.

"Something to drink, Mrs. O'hea?"

"Brandy," she answered. He nodded and moved away.

She crossed her legs, wiggled her toes and let her shoe hang from them. She closed her eyes and thought of Tucson, of Danny, of Leonard. How did they feel, after all this? I ought to call, she thought, let Shannon talk to her father and brother, let her know they're still there for her. Let's see; was it two time zones or three?

Two.

Suddenly Danny came to mind again and she realized how she missed his touch, his calm, the feel of his lips on hers. My man, Danny O'hea. Always there. She remembered playing with him and little Shannon and little Leonard, just the four of them, before Shannon had tested so good at Intersect. A picnic and Danny teasing the little ones:

"What's one plus one, Shannon?"

"Two!"

"No! Sixteen!"

And Shannon's laugh, because that was one of their little games.

Games. Now Shannon was the best gamester in the world. And yet did this game make her any happier than a joke with her father, a moment spent with her family?

I pushed her, Mrs. O'hea thought. Did I make her give up her childhood?

You gave her security. Because of Intersect she'll never know hunger.

But will she want things she cannot have?

Mrs. O'hea opened her eyes and looked over at the other mothers. They were watching her, just now, and as they did the attention of one shifted to the door. Mrs. Rinehart stood there, looking around. She stepped inside, passed close to Mrs. O'hea.

"Good afternoon, Virginia," Mrs. O'hea said. "Would you like to join me?"

Mrs. Rinehart stopped for a second, looking down.

"No," she said, and moved on to the others.

Mrs. O'hea shook her head sadly as the waiter arrived with her drink.

There was Alicia, only Alicia. For she saw, she knew. If not all then some. Some of the pain, the cruelty. Only Alicia because Alicia was Shannon's friend and she came to Shannon after the rest of the world was finished congratulating and adoring her, and when she came there was no Intersect and no people but the two of them.

Sitting, eating, talking.

"I don't know anymore," Shannon told her, and Alicia knew better than to answer right away.

Shannon went on.

"I don't know why any of this is, why we do this, what people seem to get out of it. It's such a thrill to them, to look at us, to ask and poke and demand."

Alicia nodded. It was late in the afternoon and she was tired after a difficult match. But she was smart too, and perceptive, and she could tell that she could not rest just now.

"What happens later?" she asked.

Shannon shrugged, toyed a bit with a few loose strands of hair. She was not so perfect here, not so ideal, and her hair was a mess.

"We do what they say. We dance, we play for them so they're happy."

"And that's all?"

A bitter tone crept in. "No. When we get older, they throw us away."

Alicia paused. Then she asked, "Is that what Neriah told you?"

"Sort of." And Shannon buried her face in her hands and sighed, and Alicia put her arm around her friend. She could feel Shannon beneath her hand, inhaling, exhaling, the bones of her shoulder just noticeable beneath the material of her blouse.

"What else did Neriah say?"

Shannon stirred, looked at Alicia.

"She said it was up to me."

"What is?"

"I don't know. I can't figure it out. But it's the game, Alicia. Something about the game, and it's tearing me up."

"Something in playing?"

"No. More." Shannon lowered her head again. Alicia felt her breathing quicken and she tightened her embrace, lowered her head against her friend's and began to rock slowly.

"You want me to get you something?" she asked.

"Stay," Shannon whispered. "Just stay."

Alicia nodded, raised her eyes, and looked over at the window.

Odd, it hadn't seemed so narrow before.

Dinner. The dining room; more reporters and fewer players. Glasses of water filled by waiters and waitresses in bowties, towels over their arms. Tanya, Li Yon, Maria Chavez. Sitting, chatting, smiling for the cameras. The best now, for most of the others, defeated, had gone. An Intersect championship had a flavor to it, a feeling. There was an energy at the beginning, built on anticipation, and in the middle we grew tired, just a bit, and then at the end there was more energy but of a different kind, for at the end, when you were down to the last few girls, it was the best meeting the best.

Fatima and Monique. Tshering Dem and Ellen Rodriguez. Half the final sixteen. One of these girls might be the next World Champion, folks! Stay tuned...

Shannon and Alicia.

Look!

We did.

And Shannon did not seem so perfect tonight. She was still beautiful, of course, quite so and yes indeed. But the hair was not perfect and her little dress not quite pressed and there was no bit of gloss on the lips like we were used to. And she did not walk quite so gracefully now, our Shannon, but rather like a girl who had grown too fast and was still getting used to her new body.

In fact, she seemed rather like Alicia, who had always been like that.

Shannon! Shannon! Say something!

How do you feel?

Just the enigmatic smile, a shake of the head.

They sat. Tanya looked their way and smiled. They smiled back.

We do not know what Tanya knew, what she saw, how she felt. But it is likely she sensed something in those last days. There is a suffering in many Russians, a deep pathos that we sometimes saw in her, and it is certainly fair to guess that she saw it in Shannon and Alicia, that year. She was the second best in all the world and she knew the feelings of victory and defeat and divinity.

The food came and the reporters watched. The children ate and the commentators took their notes.

Fatima seems distracted tonight. That match with Amanda Sawyer must have cost her a lot.

Amanda's a tough competitor.

This is the hard part of the competition. A lot of girls like Amanda deserve to go further.

Life isn't easy, is it?

Alicia said something to Shannon. Shannon nodded. Their plates were clean now and the waiters took them away. It grew later and the two of them talked some more, laughed a bit. Shannon looked better laughing. Her face seemed hollow, someone said later, as though she knew something was about to happen, but when she laughed that all went away. We watched as she rose, as Alicia rose, as Tanya rose. The reporters scrambled forward with questions, but none of them were answered.

Instead the Intersect girls stepped into the elevator and disappeared from view.

That night Shannon sat in her room, alone. It was late and Mother had finally gone. They had tried to call home but no one was there and Mother had promised they would try again tomorrow night.

Shannon closed her eyes and sighed, thought of Daddy and Leonard. They were fine, of course, watching the matches and knowing with pride that it was her in there.

Alone.

All, all, all alone.

Just me, with this weight I don't even understand.

Who does?

She sighed again, nodded to herself.

Ah.

She never could have called through the traditional lines. We knew it then and we know it now. Those numbers were restricted, blocked away, and you had to be very powerful or very rich or in possession of a very good reason to get them. But there are other places to get numbers, other ways, if you know how.

Shannon did. You don't play in the network and not know how things work.

Access the administrative computers, past the records division, into Public Relations. Agents, itineraries, endorsements, appearance schedules.

There.
Numbers.
Canada, Toronto metropolitan area.
There. There. Contact for photo op. Arrangements, scheduling.
Numbers.
Shannon wrote, scribbled, exited the system.
And turned to her phone.

It rang three times and then the video came on. She didn't recognize the man; he was older and his face was lined in a frown. He spoke, guarded, not quite hostile.

"Yes?"

"Neriah York, please."

His eyes narrowed. "I know you."

She nodded. He looked familiar too, but she wasn't sure from where. He spoke again.

"Shannon O'hea."

"Yes. Please, is Neriah there?"

"No. Leave us alone." His hand moved for the cutoff and Shannon tensed.

He paused.

"Why?" he asked.

She shook her head. "I don't understand."

"Why did you come? Didn't you know?"

Shannon's mouth came open but she said nothing. He spoke again.

"You play this game and you didn't know?"

"I need to talk to her. It's important."

The man's voice hardened. "Shannon O'hea, my wife is gone. I don't know what she said to you but I am sorry. Please go back to your life and leave us alone."

Shannon spoke again. "Wait…I need to talk…"

But he only hesitated at her words. Then, saying nothing, he was gone.

Chapter 16

They took him home, walked with him up to the door, rang the bell. Georgie said nothing as they did, just watched the cop as he stood, impatience on his face.

He rang the bell again. The door opened.

Mom.

She looked at the cop, at him. "Yes, officer?"

"Is this your son?"

"Yes. What's this all about?"

"He was caught at the Claremont Downtown, trying to pass off a letter to Shannon O'hea. We're here to remand him into your custody."

Mom's eyes narrowed, went from the cop to Georgie, settled there. Georgie watched her back.

"Have you had trouble of this sort before, Ma'am?" the cop asked.

She shook her head but her gaze did not change. "No. Nothing like this."

"You understand this is serious? We've had incidents this year, especially with Miss O'hea."

"Yes, yes. I'm sorry, officer. It won't happen again."

The cop nodded. "Good. Next time it goes on his record." He produced an LCD clipboard. "I need your identification and a signature."

She took the stylus, scribbled down her name, produced her purse and driver's license. When he finished with these the cop looked at Georgie again, then walked back to his car.

"Get in here," Mom said.

Dad got home. Georgie sat in the living room, staring at the vid, at the cabinets that held the VR chairs. He didn't move, not much at all, save to breathe or to blink. There was a hot spot on the back of his neck that seemed to grow as he waited, burning upward and downward. This was fear, trouble, the anticipation of the yelling and the punishment to come.

He waited as Mom talked to Dad in the kitchen, as she explained, as Dad asked something and she answered. He waited as Dad appeared, looked down at him.

He listened too, sort of.

What the hell were you doing?

You want them to think you were in on the kidnapping?

You want to be arrested? You want to go to jail?

You've got no business trying to talk to Shannon O'hea! You've got no right!

What the hell is the matter with you?

Georgie said nothing. There was nothing to say, because Dad didn't see. Maybe he couldn't or maybe he didn't want to. Whatever. But he didn't.

She's alone. I can tell, can sense it. Don't ask me how. But she's alone, all by herself, and everyone just wants to use her, and I can see it.

I can.

Days passed, and as they did Georgie watched Shannon. It was hard and it wasn't, from this distance, from home and the vid. Because even though you didn't see her much they showed a lot of old tapes of her, smiling and waving.

This is Shannon, folks. This is our girl.

He knew a lot of the scenes; he had seen them before and had watched in awe. Yet now, as he did, it was different. She was beautiful, was perfect, but there was something more to her, even in the old vids.

Love for me, Shannon.

No. Not that. Maybe if he watched the talk show again.

He did. Mom found him.

"Georgie?"

"Yeah."

"I think you've seen that enough. We had a deal, remember?"

He didn't look up. "There's something I gotta figure out."

"Put it away, Georgie. Get to your homework."

Now he turned to her. There was a look to her that he knew. With a sigh he shut off the vid.

Where is Shannon now? What is she doing? Watching maybe, looking out over the city and wondering if there is anyone out there who cares?

I do, Shannon. I do.

If they had just given her the note, she would know.

Try calling.

No. They'd never let it through.

What, then?

Georgie shook his head, looked out his window. It seemed ages ago, when she had come on the magtrain and he had seen her, or when he and the others had tried to find her in the park.

Why is everyone trying to stop me?

He looked at his poster, at her face in the yellow light thrown off by his desk lamp.

"What is it about you?" he whispered. "Why do I feel like this?"

Report cards. They weren't good, not by a long shot. An F in math and another one in civics. And a D in English, just barely. Absences, too, a lot of them. Stern looks on his teachers' faces as they handed the cards out, then the usual instructions.

Take them home and have your parents sign them.

He did, leaving the cards on the kitchen table where Mom and Dad would see them. There would be trouble for the grades, probably another lecture and maybe some yelling, but none of this was important just now.

No. Just now there was Shannon, the mystery of her that he had to solve. About the game, what that was, what that meant.

Is Shannon the game? I watch her on the VR and it is her, so completely, so honestly.

Just what I want her to be.

Exactly what I want her to be.

Is this important?

Is she what everyone else wants her to be?

How is that possible?

He heard the front door open, heard someone come in. Voices. Georgie looked at the poster, stared at it. How can you be what everyone wants you to be? Everyone is different. They want different things.

What is it about you, Shannon? How can you give everyone something different with the same moves? And what does it do to you, giving everything like that? What do we give you in return?

He sensed it then, in that calm in his room, cut off and alone. Something he had known all along but hadn't seen. It isn't giving anymore. No. Giving comes from within. It is not and should not be expected, required.

Like we do. We all get what we want from Shannon because we take it. We, you and I and Mom and Dad and the sportscasters and the world. Shannon was ours, our girl, a thing we used.

Love for me, Shannon.

For me.

A knock. Georgie looked over at his door.

"Georgie? Can I come in?"

Dad. Georgie pushed back from his desk.

"Okay."

The door opened.

Dad was a big man, built on a strong frame. He had a flat, gentle face and eyes that seemed just a bit too far apart. You could tell he was Georgie's father by the face, by the look they each had.

Georgie watched him as he stepped inside.

"How are you, son?"

"Fine, Dad."

Dad nodded, looked around the room. His gaze rested for a moment on the poster of Shannon O'hea and then he looked back at his son.

"What's going on with school, Georgie? You sick?"

"I don't know."

"You don't know." Dad looked around again, pushed his hands into his pockets. "This is your worst report card yet, Georgie. They're going to hold you back a year if you don't get better. Do you understand?"

"Yeah, Dad."

"Is that all you have to say?"

"What else do you want?"

"I want you to think, Georgie. You're a bright boy and you can do better than this. Your mother and I have been talking; is it the game?"

Georgie looked down. "No. Not anymore."

"Then what is it?"

"I got important things to think about."

"What things?"

"You wouldn't understand."

Again Dad's eyes settled on the poster. "You've been watching a lot of vid, haven't you?"

Georgie nodded.

"Is it something to do with the vid? Georgie—"

"Leave me alone!"

The words came out quick, before he could stop them. Snapped, spat, like bullets. Dad went silent for a moment. Then he stepped forward, reached down to Georgie's desk and picked up the book that lay there. "Intersect," he said. "That is it, isn't it?"

Heat rose, up through Georgie's collar, to his face. He shook his head.

"No."

"Then why did they arrest you at the hotel?"

Georgie shook his head violently. "You don't understand. You don't get it."

"You're throwing away your future for this game, Georgie!"

"You watch it too!"

The cry was half accusation, half confession. Dad looked down at him and his face was stern.

"Son, I don't watch it at work."

"But you watch!"

The man nodded. "Yes. I'm going to keep this book, Georgie, until your grades are better. Then you can have it back, understand?"

Georgie jumped up. "No!"

Dad stepped over to the poster, pulled it down.

"This too," he said.

"No!"

"And no more vid and no more VR. Am I making myself clear?"

Georgie stopped in mid-breath. His hands were at his sides, clenched. This was wrong, cruel, and he could feel the rage building in him, impotent, vicious rage.

"No!" he shouted. "No!"

His father shouted back: "That is enough, Georgie!"

"You got no right!"

"I have no right?" And then it was terror, for the man took the poster, and ripped it clean in half, then again in quarters, and in eighths. And he threw the shards to the floor in contempt.

"I am your father and you will do as I say!"

"You got no right!"

"I have every right! Now you get to your homework!"

He slammed the door as he left and Georgie did not move. Instead he watched the floor, stared down at the pieces of paper scattered there, at his Shannon, torn, broken. And Georgie went to his knees as the first tears rose, touched at the torn remains of the poster, at the section of her face, the half of her smile.

"I'll help you, Shannon," he swore. "I will I will I will."

Chapter 17

Li Yon lasted a full twelve minutes.

These were the final days, the final games. Impossible wonders, from the little blonde girl from Tucson, and the words of billions, spread by the vids, began to change.

New things.

Did you see it?

She's too good. Not fair.

I know. But they've checked. You can't cheat on the network. She has something, something special. More than love, more than joy. Something else she's feeling, and nobody can defend against it.

Then why have her compete?

What do you mean?

Couldn't she do this alone? Just her, in the matrices. Every day, maybe, in the afternoon, and we could all watch.

That's a thought.

Of course, it wouldn't be a game anymore.

Who cares? I just want Shannon.

Shannon.

Shannon.

Eight now. Three more rounds. And in the quiet, empty halls of the hotel, they watched one another. And we watched, and their mothers and Matrons, and the administrators and the publicity people.

Tanya, Monica, Shannon, Alicia, Fatima, Monique, Ellen and Charlene.

Remember? The courtesies, the false smiles at the table? The fears as the matches approached?

The secret thoughts? The quiet meetings as mothers tucked their little girls in for bed?

"Alicia?"

"Yeah?"

Quiet in the dimness.

"Why Shannon?"

"Huh?"

"What is it about her? What does she do for you?"

"She's my best friend, Mom."

Mrs. Rinehart sighed. She laid her daughter's hand in hers and gripped it tightly. It wasn't a quick thing, this thought; in truth she didn't know when it had begun, when she had first noticed.

Shannon. She was it. She was why. Alicia wasn't quite her Alicia anymore, and only a few days remained now.

Monica Chavez, then probably Tanya Kirilova, then Shannon in the finals.

Shannon, Alicia's friend. Unhealthy. A bad influence. That's what it was, really. Too much time together and that meant sympathy and probably a slip, a bit of compassion in the wrong place.

Alicia beat her before. She can if she wants to.

But remember the dinner afterwards?

Not healthy.

"Mom?"

Mom. And Shannon has a mother too, distant, like ice. Probably telling her these same things.

"Alicia, I'm worried."

"Why?"

"What is it with Shannon?"

Alicia went silent. People like the O'heas want us, Mrs. Rinehart thought. They need us. Without us they have nothing to be better than, no place in the world.

"I think she's scared," Alicia said.

"Why?"

"I don't know. I wish I could help her, though."

Mrs. Rinehart looked down at her daughter. She could just see her face, framed in the black of her hair on the pillow. And the words came naturally and without thought.

"Perhaps she is afraid of you."

"Why?"

"You beat her, Alicia. You are the only one who could. She wants to be champion and you are in the way."

"I don't think it's me."

"I do. Maybe you should keep your distance, at least for a few days."

"What if she gets mad at me?"

"It's only a few days, Alicia. Just until the end of the tournament. All right?"

Alicia went silent, closed her eyes. Her mother watched her and squeezed her hand. "Three more matches," she said to her. "You can do it."

Nothing. Mrs. Rinehart rose.

"Goodnight, honey. I love you."

Tanya, Shannon, Alicia and Fatima.

And the vids seemed silent for a time.

Were we tired, or resting as we waited? There were days to pass before the semifinals, hours and minutes so the girls could prepare, hours and minutes so the endorsements could be made and the sponsors appeased, so our appetites could be whetted.

So we could think about it.

Tanya, Shannon, Alicia and Fatima.

Russian, American, American and Iraqi.

Eastern Orthodox, Presbyterian, American Agnostic and Shiite Muslim.

Brunette, Blonde, Brunette, Brunette.

Four at the table, four so far apart.

And the day approached, day by day.

Semifinals on Saturday, then the final matches on Sunday.

Predictions?

Vegas says Shannon, Tanya, Alicia, Fatima. Atlantic City says Alicia will upset, get at least second.

How about you?

What did you think?

Thursday. Friday.

Watch the vids.

Shannon with Alicia but they don't say much. This is Moscow again, with the rumors, the whispering, the speculation. The vids are back now and they won't be quiet. Every move, every gesture, every hair and every stitch of their clothing is watched, analyzed. Look at how Alicia is dressed! Will Shannon wear that diamond necklace again?

Oh, I hope so.

Yes, I hope so.

And what are they thinking? What do they see in each other? How will Tanya do?

What do you say, Shannon?

What do you say?

Go back. Watch her turn, away from the mike, and watch her face. Watch as she speaks to Alicia, as she smiles and her friend smiles too, as though there is something they know that we don't, as though they are sharing some private joke at our expense.

Alicia! Shannon! What?

Go back.

Remember.

Shannon alone, up in her room. Thirteen now, defending World Champion. A quick conversation with Daddy and Leonard fresh in her mind.

"Good luck, Honey. We know you can do it."

"Go for it, Shannon."

For what? Why?

"We love you, Shannon."

Do you?

Can you?

What is love?

She rose, paced for a moment. Mother was gone now, in the room next door, so close. Alicia was down the hall and Tanya was a bit further. Fatima was the other direction.

I should prepare.

Why?

You want to win, don't you?

She nodded to herself. But will I?

What is it, to win? What does it mean?

Go back. What did it mean in Moscow?

Joy. And people wanting you, and loving you, and writing letters to you. Listening to you talk about anything, just to hear you. Why is it so important? I'm just me; I'm just good at Intersect. I can't paint or draw or act.

I have nothing else, but this is nothing too.

Was that what Neriah meant?

Darkness came and the city slept, anticipating.

Saturday. Shannon and Fatima. Were you among the four billion who would watch? Did you set aside the time, cancel something with your children, ignore your mother or your father?

Shannon and Fatima.

Shannon arrived early; Fatima also. They walked into the museum, up to the upper level. Below, the reporters scrambled for a shot, for a moment at the microphones. Would they speak?

Not Fatima. She never does.

Shannon?

No.

How does she look? Is she ready?

It's six PM in Baghdad. They've been waiting all day for this.

Seven AM in Tucson.

Let's go to Jeff in the museum. I think he's got a few words before this starts.

Shannon went to her interface chamber, sat. It was quiet in here, empty save for the VR chair and the little shelf and the stool beside it. A place to concentrate, to sweat, to fear. But she felt none of this now. Instead she was empty, like the room itself, hollow, for that was the key.

Be hollow, open. Do not erect barriers but build bridges. And when the time comes let it all out; the good, the bad, everything. Make constructs out of more than love but out of what it is to be you, to be human.

They can't defend against those, for with only love, they are incomplete in the network.

You are whole.

You are Shannon O'hea.

The call came through.

"O'hea, Al-Hakim."

Shannon rose, settled into the VR chair. It came to life and she allowed herself to descend into the first matrix. Numbers came and she wrapped these around herself to prepare, waiting.

Waiting.

And Fatima came.

There was a power to her, something new. Shannon dodged, maneuvered, extended. Feelings grew in her, new places inside, new sensations as she struck back with a derivative of the square root of pi.

Five minutes and the world sighed.
Ten and the world wept.
Fifteen. Shannon! Shannon!
Twenty and it was done.

Did you sense it then? Did you watch and feel for the first time? That touch, that bit of something. Not quite love, not quite joy, like an apple that is not sweet but is sour. Sour, tempting, different.

That was Shannon against Fatima Al-Hakim.

It had been there before, against Cathy Nesbitt, against Li Yon, against Monique Armeneau. Just that taste of something dangerous, spicy. Something new to Shannon that no one thought to consider.

Was that it? Was that what made her unbeatable?

Perhaps. But remember now the second semifinal. Remember now Tanya and Alicia.

Remember.

They came to the museum. There was still a tension in the air, a sensation transmitted through the vid to every corner of the world, to every receiver and VR chair, where the billions waited.

Remember.

Up the stairs, through the main doors. The crowd outside, shouting and cheering. Which of these girls would challenge Shannon for her crown? Which would battle Fatima for the bronze?

Remember.

Alicia and her Matron, into her interface chamber. Tanya and hers inside. Settling in, words hushed among the reporters, talking to the distant broadcast booths. Setting up, bringing things on line, descending.

Down. Settling, preparing.

Across the way, Tanya.

A pirouette as it began, a strike. Tanya turned and rose and with her rose a billion bytes from a million lines of data.

Last year! Last year! Remember!
Turn! Dance!
And Alicia did.
And we awed.
Tanya lashed again, grace and glory. A turn, a rhythm, a step.
Five minutes.
Watch her.

Careful.
Now!
And Tanya dodged, perfect, ideal.
Ten minutes.
Strike with irrationals, with flaws in flawless logic, with the geometry of beauty and impossibility. Tanya blocked, turned again; Alicia moved, side-stepped in joy.
Twenty minutes.
Laugh. Sing.
Thirty minutes.
Meeting, perfection. Intersect.
Forty minutes.
There.
Were you watching?
That was the point. Perfect point, perfect joining. You and it, Alicia, you and the machine that is now you. You and the machine that is in you, that is your mind, that is your being. Filling, reacting, redefining.
Changing everything you are, Alicia. An eternal loop: line one, go to line two. Line two, go to line one.
Forever and ever, Amen.
Tanya saw it first; she could, for she was in there, deep in the matrices with Alicia, moving, turning. Alicia slipping away, into nonbeing, into the endless loop, the endless pirouette, the endless fall. Slipping, slipping.
And Tanya reacted. Algorithms fell away, her defenses dropped, collapsed. Jumping forward in her own abstract unbeing, reaching for the girl who was falling away.
We saw, then.
Oh God!
Alicia! Alicia!
Turning, spinning and cannot stop. Looping, around and around and around. You! It! You! It!
Tanya was there, reaching in with hands that extended through the matrices, through the unreal world of fiber optics and connections and switches. Reaching in, pulling, shrieking.
Get her out! Get her out!
And then, in that second, Alicia's Matron jumping up, the door to the chamber snapping open, technicians rushing in and shutting off the VR connection.
And within Alicia, the unreal pirouette, spinning and spinning forever.

Chapter 18

Evening. Quiet.

In the cities and in the homes, we waited.

News. Anything.

How is she? What happened?

Software loop. Excess feedback, overload. The human brain has only so many neurons and they can only do so much at once.

Is she dead?

No. Not really. Heard the mother went into shock.

Remember?

Evening, quiet, as we waited.

Tanya was the official winner; she held the matrices in the end. She would face Shannon tomorrow and Fatima would get the bronze by default. But there was none of Moscow here, not this time. No, just a hurried trip back to the hotel for Tanya, a rush up to the guarded floor. No words, no comments. We had seen what she had tried to do, how she had risked herself to try and save Alicia.

A few of us, in our quiet shock, whispered a thank you.

Nothing more.

Look at me now and listen. It was a risk. It came with the game and it was a part of the game. Intersect was not unique in this; how many bodies and souls have been broken by football, by rugby, by boxing? You know this. You know that this is part of the thrill, that there is a high to living on the edge, to tempting the devil. And in truth Intersect was safer than those other sports, that the risk was low and that for the joy we received, it was worth it.

Of course. Remember?

Go back now, to Chicago. To that night. To those who remained, who had not yet flown home, as they gathered in the hotel lobby and silently boarded a bus. Reporters watching, vids rolling, but silence now, no shouted questions, no pushing, no motion at all.

And silently the bus moving away.

They let them in, the little group, and the doctors and the nurses watched and shook their heads and wondered how such little girls could dance in the matrices as they did. Past the main doors, past Admitting and down the hall to the elevator. Up then, up and up, past floor and floor, past those who would live and those who would die, past cancer and heart disease and AIDS, up and up to the secure ward on the top floor where the Vice President had once had his prostate surgery. And in the elevator the girls stood close together, not so old now, not so aloof and mature.

Li Yon whispered something to Tanya, glanced at Shannon. Tanya whispered something back and Shannon saw the both of them nod.

She said nothing. The elevator doors opened and they stepped outside. A nurse met them.

"This way."

They went. Quietly, down the hall, to a door.

"She's sleeping now. Please be quiet."

The door opened. In a line they stepped inside; in a line they filed to the bedside and stared.

Alicia.

On her back, eyes closed, mouth just open so they could see her little white teeth. Breathing slowly, in and out, almost peaceful there, like a princess waiting for a kiss. Waiting, waiting. And falling, forever.

The girls watched, not children, not the innocents we saw and loved. Rather, adults, mature and aware of what this was, what had happened and how. Tanya's face, drawn, tight, for she had been the one who saw it happen, who had been right there. Fatima, dark in shadow, looking down. Li Yon, Maria Chavez, Ellen Rodriguez. Standing, looking.

Shannon, between Tanya and Maria. This you cannot see, cannot know. There are no vids of this, no records. Shannon, watching her friend. Shannon, with the others, standing silently, knowing that the nurses were watching too, that they were wondering what it meant, what it was.

And seeing as each of the girls, one after another, touched Alicia on the forehead and moved slowly for the door.

For every sport, every subculture, no matter how small, has its traditions and its rituals.

At last only Shannon remained. She stood by the bed, extended her finger to emulate her peers, but hesitated, pulled back, held suddenly rigid. Tanya appeared again, touched her arm.

"We must go, Shannon," she said in broken English.

"Later."

Tanya hesitated, nodded. Then she moved to the nurse, whispered something to her.

The nurse nodded and left with her. The door slid closed.

And still Shannon stood.

Alicia inhaled, exhaled.

Shannon remembered.

She remembered when Alicia had beaten her, how beautiful the last moves had been, how she had hesitated at the poetry of it, the gentle, patient rhythms. How seeing her own works cut and sliced and brought down had been a great joy in itself. And she knew, at last, why this was. It was no strategy by Alicia that had done this, no plan. No. It was Alicia herself, her love and her art.

Alicia the dancer.

But there was more than that.

Alicia with the ice cream, licking the spoon. Alicia talking and laughing at the Russian vid. Alicia in her arms, buried in her embrace, weeping. Alicia listening when no one else would.

Alicia her friend.

Shannon sighed, closed her eyes, let her head fall forward. A moment passed, then another. She was not aware of this, of how the clock on the wall counted off the seconds, the minutes.

Someone came in behind her. She turned.

A doctor stood there, neat in his lab coat, a clipboard under one arm. His hair was thinning with middle age and the beginnings of wrinkles showed on his face.

He walked to the bedside, lifted Alicia's arm to take her pulse off the watch on his wrist.

"Doctor..." Shannon whispered.

He looked over at her, his gaze sharp and unfriendly.

"You're O'hea, aren't you?"

She nodded.

"Your friends have gone. Call for a limo when you leave." He turned his attention back to Alicia.

"Doctor, I have to know…"

"Know what, O'hea? You play in the matrices. You know this is a risk."

"Not this," she protested. "This was a one in a million thing—"

"There are still risks, O'hea. That's part of the appeal, isn't it?" His words were iced with scorn.

Shannon said nothing. Her little hands formed fists and she felt her chest tighten. Tighten and tighten until she felt it ready to explode. Only then did she sense the first wet tears running down her cheeks.

The doctor glanced at her and saw. He spoke again.

"Mother and dad are in the next room," he said. "Had to sedate her and he's finally sleeping too. They're as bad as she is."

Shannon looked up, her gaze sharp. The doctor raised Alicia's arm a bit further, released it. It held in place. He guided it back down.

"How…?" Shannon began.

"She's alive. Right now that's about all."

"Doctor…"

"We don't know yet."

Shannon looked down. She should go, should walk out the door and go back to the hotel and get some sleep for tomorrow. Tanya would be tough and this was for everything.

She turned, stepped toward the door.

Everything.

"O'hea?" the doctor asked.

"Yes?"

"Wait."

She faced him again. His eyes had changed somehow; nothing obvious, nothing certain. But changed. His voice was softer too.

"Don't go, O'hea."

She tilted her head, extended a hand and closed it on the rail of the bed. The doctor spoke again.

"I have a daughter."

Nothing. Alicia breathed. A machine made a noise.

"She is twelve years old. She worships you, did you know that? Everything about you. Everything you are, and everything she thinks you are. She wants to be you."

He reached out, just touched Shannon's cheek with his forefinger, felt the wetness of a tear.

"She tested, O'hea. School team. Now she plays and won't talk about anything else. She sees you and thinks it's the easy life, and I can't tell her that for every Shannon O'hea there are a million girls who are not and who waste the best years of their lives trying to be Shannon O'hea."

His finger drew away and his voice hardened just a bit.

"You think it's easy to be a father when you're up against Shannon O'hea?"

Slowly, Shannon shook her head. The doctor turned back toward the bed, glanced at his clipboard. He did not face her as he spoke again.

"Come on," he said. "Let's get her up and walk her a bit. She'll follow if we give her a lead."

"All right."

They raised Alicia up, stood her. The doctor produced a hospital robe and they pulled it over Alicia's shoulders. He took her right hand and indicated that Shannon should take her left.

"That's good. Now, gently pull her forward."

Alicia took a step as they did.

"Talk to her, O'hea. It can't hurt."

"What should I say?"

"Anything. There may still be something in there."

Shannon paused, looked at Alicia. Her friend stared straight ahead, her mouth just open.

"Alicia?" she asked.

Nothing.

"Alicia, please be all right."

They reached the edge of the room, turned back around. Alicia stepped as they pulled, clumsy, one foot and then another. Shannon tried to speak again but her voice cracked and she grew quiet.

"That's all right," the doctor said. "Just hold her hand if that's all you can do. She'll understand."

They walked. Around and around the room. Five minutes. Ten. Fifteen. And Shannon could not help but notice her friend's bony knees, her little wrists and rigid hands. Alicia's eyes were open now, but they stared straight ahead and did not react when the doctor passed his hand in front of them. When they finally put her back into the bed he turned to Shannon one last time.

"She may recover, in time," he said. "Or she may be like this for the rest of her life. More likely she'll be somewhere in between. You want some advice, O'hea? Don't go tomorrow. Don't compete. Stay here with your friend instead. You're too young and you've got too much of life ahead of you to take chances like this."

Shannon said nothing. She looked down at Alicia, touched at the hospital sheet. "I'd like to be alone for a little while," she said.

"All right."

He pulled up a chair for her and left.

Shannon sat, rested her head against the bedrail. She said nothing, only felt as the metal grew warm against her forehead.

A moment passed. Alicia's breathing paused, resumed. Regular, like the second hand of a clock.

Outside, we waited.

Midnight came and went.

Dance for me, Alicia.

Spin for me, Tanya.

Love for me, Shannon.

Shannon raised her head. She looked around the darkened room.

And she began to see.

It had been there all the time. All the time going back, ever since that first moment on that first day. In their eyes, their voices, hidden subtly in their words. The way the funny looking man had first looked at her so long ago.

This isn't for you, Shannon.

None of it is yours. None, not at all. Not the clothes, not the toys, not the jewelry. No. You are ours, Shannon. We need you, we bought you, and we own you. You and all you are.

Even Sydney, Cairo, and Moscow.

They are for us.

A wave shot through her, a shudder, a moan. Her legs went weak and she gripped the bedrail to keep from falling from the chair. She moaned again, loud now, the sound growing in pitch until it was a whimper, pounding again and again from her lungs. And then her arms grew weak too and she settled to the floor beside the bed, brought her knees up and held them against her, rocking back and forth, back and forth. Hair fell into her eyes, ragged, unkempt, lost.

Love for us, Shannon.

You are what we think you are.

Intersect.

And she saw and she knew. Everything was for them, for the anonymous billions who watched her, who bought Kleen-Smile and Zip Cola because she told them to. Because she was a name and a face someone could make a million dollars off of. Because it was easier to sit in a VR chair and feel imaginary pride in an imaginary her than it was to feel pride in themselves. Imaginary pride, imaginary love.

Loving what they thought she was. Loving what they made her.
Shannon rose, moved to the foot of Alicia's bed, stared at her friend.
Love me, Shannon.
Remember?
Me?

Alicia.
Yes.
Because Alicia was different. In all the world she was unique, the one thing not given, not contracted, bought, paid for. No. Alicia was a knock on the door in Moscow, a knock we did not approve of, did not condone or sanction. Alicia was Shannon's friend because she was Shannon's friend, and she was unspoiled by money or fame or expectations.
Invaluable in a world that was afraid.
And now the game had taken that away.
Intersect.
Intersect.
Love for me, Shannon. Win the championship for America, Shannon. Sign here, Shannon. Smile, Shannon. Wave, Shannon. Wear this blouse, Shannon.
Obey, Shannon. You are not important. Only what we think you are is important. Win for us because we cannot win for ourselves.
Do it!
And you will be doomed.
Who am I, if I'm not Shannon O'hea? What am I? What will I do if not Intersect? What is there in my life for me?
Over her head, Alicia stirred. Shannon tensed, leaned forward.
Nothing. She watched for a moment.
And her own voice returned to her.
If you win this title, they win. And if you lose, they will still win.
Why?
Because you will have still played. You will have obeyed. You will have been their Shannon O'hea, not your own.
How, then, can I be me?
What is me?
She shuddered again because she suddenly knew.

A voice, ragged with hate.
There is a way.

Chapter 19

Outside, we waited. We, you and I, and the fans and the sportscasters and the public. For it was not over yet, not by a long shot. Shannon was still America's best chance: still the favorite, still the darling, still the heroine. Our girl, America's girl.

Still at the hospital as dawn broke. Today is the day, folks! A rematch from Moscow. Shannon and Tanya. The best in the world.

What's that? She's emerged? She's out, heading for the hotel?

Yes, yes. That's confirmed, Jeff. The limo just left.

What did she say?

Nothing. Not a word.

What's the status of Alicia, then? Let's go live to the hospital. Pat?

I'm here, Tom. We've got her doctor. Doctor? How is she?

Undetermined levels of damage to the brain. We are still uncertain as to the prognosis for recovery.

But it looks bad, doesn't it, Doctor? A real tragedy, yes?

The vid shows it all. Look closely: the doctor's face, drawn, just a bit irritated at the reporter's tone. Looking at her and answering slowly.

I would say that tragedy is an understatement.

What about Shannon O'hea, doctor? She spent the night here; did she say anything to you?

Again the pause, the look, the face.

No.

No.

Remember Georgie now. He was at home, and Mom and Dad were watching the vid and he was watching too and they seemed to have forgotten, for the moment at least, that he wasn't supposed to. Watching the vid as all America watched, as all the world watched, with mute, sadistic fascination about a twelve year old girl who would never dance for us again.

That's all from here, Tom.

Well. Fine.

And Georgie's mother saying, "What a shame. She could have won it."

And his father: "Now it's up to Shannon."

And Georgie himself, lowering his head, closing his eyes. What does a boy think, when he worships a girl? How do you quantify blind, foolish, adolescent passion? How do you predict what he will do for her?

How, when he in fact is more than just this? How, when his eyes are open and he can see what none of us would?

You cannot. Don't try. The experts did, later, when they tried to reconstruct it all, when they and their computers and psych models and theories all worked to solve the puzzle and failed. For there is no predicting a Georgie, no way of knowing what he will do. He was silent now, thinking. The match was in six hours; there was time, if he could act. The crowds would be thin, too, because this was the world championship match and everyone would be at home in their VR chairs.

Thin enough? Maybe.

To do what? Georgie opened his eyes.

Take a chance, ride a star.

Oh, Shannon. What if it happens to you too?

Then it came to him. Slowly, not suddenly, but inexorable. He could not stop it any more than he could stop the sun from shining. A growing feeling, a building realization. And as it came to him Georgie looked over at his parents, still sitting glued to the vid, and he saw them, perhaps for the first time, as they really were. Them, the Joneses, the Riveras. Everyone, almost. Everyone who sat in front of their vids and who slipped into their VR chairs to watch their little princesses do battle with love. Because that was really it, wasn't it? They loved Shannon; it was in every turn of their heads as she passed, every impulse to watch her, to follow her, to swim in the warm sea of her soul.

Will she smile at me?

Oh, I hope so.

Yes, I hope so.

Georgie tried to call that love, tried to feel its familiar burning within himself. He tried to shiver as he had before, looking up at her poster and her mysterious smile, and he tried to call upon the feelings he had had when he and a billion others had danced with her in the matrices. He tried, hard, and failed, and saw.

He loved Mom and Dad. He loved his grandmothers and his grandfathers, and aunt Bethany and aunt Miriam and his uncle Jonathan. And he loved his two cousins in Montana and his other two in Missouri and yes, he loved Jim and he loved Adam. And as Georgie stood and as Georgie watched he knew then what he was seeing and what he was hearing, and he thought of Shannon and he tried again to call on the old familiar feelings.

Again he failed.

There was no denying it anymore.

He did not love Shannon O'hea.

He could not, and why was clear. He did not know her. Georgie saw now, as another commercial came on the vid, why he loved and how he loved. He saw the time, the months and the years, where love grew and prospered. And Georgie saw the wholeness of it, of love, and that love was more than the sudden, impossible pleasure of the game, that it was the whole of you and the whole of them, not the part you show, but more, deep down, than is seen. Love was acceptance of their whole and once it was real there could be no compromise in it, no conditions, no demands. The words came, in his mind, true and certain, and with them came a sudden honest relief, as though someone had lifted a weight and a haze from his soul.

I do not love you.

I do not know you.

You are distant.

Shannon was a face, only, on the vid. She was a soul, only, on the network. She was a stranger who had never seen his face.

They were going on on the vid, talking, analyzing. There was a lot of footage from last year, comparisons being made and debated.

Shannon won't be able to use that move this year. Tanya's tougher and she'll block it.

How about the new stuff?

Hard to say; Tanya's never faced it before. I'm just as curious about Alicia.

You think it'll affect Shannon?

Might affect Tanya. She was in there when it happened.

True. Let's take a break.

An ad came on and Dad muted it, stretched in his chair. He and Mom started talking again and Georgie continued to watch them. His feet were getting tired from standing but he was afraid to move forward and sit. There was an emptiness inside him where so much had been before, a hollowness that made him fear he would cease to be. And there was a wrongness, too, that he could not locate, could not pinpoint or isolate. The ad ended and the familiar faces returned.

What about Shannon? Any word?

Nothing. They limoed her back this morning. She had breakfast in her room. I suppose she's getting ready.

I'll bet she regrets having that friendship now.

The second man nodded, just a bit, in his clean, perfect suit, his ruggedly handsome features forming a bit of a smile. A knowing smile; an I-told-you-so smile.

Georgie looked down, away from the screen of the vid. He had to move, suddenly. Not just to fidget, or to pace in his room and wonder what he should do, but to move, to act. The wrongness had taken on a form, a focus. Bearing down, targeting a single soul.

Shannon O'hea.

Everyone who loves her. What I was.

Georgie turned in a deliberate motion, stepped into his room. He emerged with his coat on and when he did Dad was facing him.

"I've talked it over with your mother, Georgie. This'll be the match of the century, they say, and we don't think it's fair to cut you off. If you like, you can watch it."

Georgie looked at his father, closely. The man said nothing, and deep in his gut Georgie felt the urge, the beauty, the need. His Shannon, playing like she had never played before, loving him, for him, to him. But Georgie knew, deep inside, that this was nothing. It was not Shannon they loved, and it was not love that they gave or that they took. It was a facade, a fantasy; it was the truth of Intersect. Taking, not giving, because in the network he and Mom and Dad and the Joneses and the Riveras and all the billions of us did not honestly return her love, could not.

We did not know her, and despite all its glories, love was not something Intersect could do.

He shook his head, zipped up his coat as his father watched.

"No thanks. I gotta go."

And Georgie turned and walked away.

Chapter 20

▼

No.

The pause, the look, the face.

That's all it took. The right pause, the right look. Silence at the right time, when everyone was still in a bit of a daze, still a bit shocked. Silence when we needed more.

Silence that we filled that Sunday morning.

Rumors.

They built, growing among a world eager for some relief, flashing at the speed of light across continents, drawing the attentions of billions. One voice, talking to another, across a table or across an ocean. Spreading to others, to the vid stations, to the networks. Spreading, from English to Chinese to Japanese, to Russian, to Arabic and to French and to Swahili and to Spanish. Voices, talking, speculating.

She will dedicate this triumph to the memory of her friend.

Arabic to Hebrew and to Farsi, Russian to Kazakh to Uzbek, Chinese to Japanese to Hindi to Indonesian. Spanish to Portuguese and French to German and Dutch and Norwegian.

Tune in this afternoon. She'll rewrite the record books. Motivation, that's it. It's what makes champions.

Commentators and announcers, caught up in the growing flow, the growing excitement, saying and predicting impossible things that today, at least, seemed possible after all.

Once in a lifetime, that's what it is. It'll make Moscow look like a picnic, the first championship at Sydney like a practice. Watch it! Watch it, whatever you do!

She's the best that's ever been. You'll never see anything like this again. Not in a hundred years!

Never again! Never!

Tune in!

Watch!

This you cannot forget.

Inside the hotel, Shannon sat quietly in her room. Mother had come in a little while ago, had put an arm around her and had kissed her gently on the forehead. She had sat with her, not speaking, not moving, for some time.

Then: "Shannon?"

Shannon looked up.

"Shannon, are you going to be all right? This is important."

Shannon nodded slowly. "I'm all right."

"You're sure? Because if you have any doubt, if you are afraid to go, you tell me. We stop this whole thing right now and get on a plane and go home."

Shannon watched her mother. There was a numbness to it all, like the whole world was filled with soft cotton and she had to wade through it. It had been there last night, when she had sat in the chair beside Alicia and had tried to sleep a bit, and this morning when she had finally left her. Fuzz, static in everything, blinding all but the certain.

"No," she said. "I have to do it."

Mother nodded, held her tightly.

"Do you want me to come with you?"

"No. You have to stay here."

Mother said nothing. Finally she rose and went to check on things with Shannon's Matron.

Shannon prepared. She took a hot shower, washed her hair. When she emerged she toweled herself dry and changed slowly into her white panties and white tights and white leotard. She put on her shoes one at a time, laced them up with a long tested series of pulls. Quietly she put on her shining blue warmups.

And outside, by the billions, people moved to their VR chairs.

Shannon sat before her mirror, stared for a moment at her reflection. Then she took out her brush, began stroking her hair. Pulling, pulling, teasing the strands into place, reaching for her curler and adding just a bit of body, just a bit of bounce. Her face then; a touch of blush, a hint of mascara, a trace of gloss on the lips.

Making more of what she had, enough to be noticed but not seen. Perfection.

She rose and stepped into the hall. It was empty now, quiet. As she moved forward the words came again and again and with them came the fear.

There is a way.

If you play, you are what they want you to be. Your life is what they make it. Even if you lose nothing will change, and there will be more Shannons and Alicias tomorrow, and people will own them the way they own you.

Billions more moved, settling in, waiting.

Spin for me, Tanya.

Love for me, Shannon.

Almost time. Tanya is already at the Museum. Shannon should be coming out any minute now. There's a small crowd outside the hotel, waiting to wish her well.

She walked down the hall and to the elevator. The guard smiled as she passed and she smiled back at him, stared for a moment.

Then down, past floor after floor, to the lobby.

Security met her there. Big men, strong men behind dark glasses. Scanners sweeping ahead, hands near weapons, ready to draw.

They said nothing as she walked forward.

Outside, the crowd waited, straining to become a part of history. Cameras panned over them, sending their images off satellites a hundred miles overhead, beaming them across the world.

This should be it, any minute now. I understand she's in the lobby. The crowd is moving but they're orderly. Must be real fans, to be here instead of in a VR chair...

Remember? Did you look at the images, the movement, the crowd? Bodies, people, straining for their Shannon, crying her name? Look closely, hard.

And see.

For there, in the front, stood Georgie.

Look again. He is not like the others. Look at his face, if you can. Calm, almost serene, gentle. Look at his body, at the way he does not move with the crowd, does not cry out. Hands in his pockets, eyes open, just watching, waiting.

As she emerges.

"Shannon!" someone screamed, and the crowd erupted with noise. "We love you, Shannon! We love you!"

She stepped forward, toward the waiting limousine. Georgie did not move, his legs and belly pressed by the crowd against the police barricade, his hands still in his pockets. Still he said nothing, only watched her as she passed him, as her eyes scanned over him.

What was he thinking? How much did he know? What did he suspect?

Why was it him?

"Shannon!" the crowd screamed again.

And she paused.

There is no reason why she did, just then. Perhaps, though, when she saw Georgie, she saw something more. Something different, unique. Perhaps that he did not scream struck her somehow, went past her guard.

She turned, stepped back, toward the crowd.

One of the security men moved to block her.

Georgie froze in place. The vid shows his mouth, just open, his face still calm, his eyes still gentle. It is not an image you can forget.

Shannon stopped, facing him from less than two meters, and she extended a hand.

"Come," she said to him.

Chapter 21

Did you watch?

Did you see?

Remember now? This is why you are here, why you have come, why you have listened. Remember the vids, the taste in the air, the great wonder at it all? The final game, the greatest game?

Where were you?

Did you see?

How Georgie stepped forward, how the camera caught his face, how the security man hesitated and then ran his scanner over him? How Shannon stood, so perfectly still, so calm, so beautiful? The sigh of the crowd as she spoke again?

"Come."

Another step. The security man whispering into his radio. His voice, stressed, asking what to do, how to handle it.

Answer: I don't know. Is he clean?

Yeah.

Frisk him. What the hell is she doing?

Hands out, patting Georgie down. Arms, chest, back, groin, legs.

Nothing on him. What now?

What does she want?

The security man looked back at Shannon and she spoke to Georgie again, her voice soft, perfect.

"Come."

We sighed, at the sound. And across the vid lines, across the world, we watched in awe.

All right. All right. Let him go. But I want you in the car with them. Keep an eye, keep an eye. If this goes wrong...

I know.

The security man stepped back. Georgie raised his hand to Shannon's. Fingers met, closed about each other. Her hand, perfect, white, small, in his, holding him. Her face, gentle, watching his.

Shannon smiled.

A sigh again, around the world. She and he, stepping to the limo, the guard behind, hand beneath his coat, on the hilt of his weapon, ready. The door opening and them sliding inside, the guard close. The door closing and the vehicle speeding away.

She held Georgie's hand as they sat. He was watching her and he was afraid and he wondered if she could hear the pounding of his heart.

"What's your name?" she asked.

He told her and wished suddenly that he had said George instead.

"Georgie. I like that. I'm Shannon, Georgie."

He took in a deep breath, let it out. She could feel his hand tremble, and she tightened her hold.

"It's all right, Georgie."

He swallowed, inhaled again. And he said:

"I know."

"Good."

They were moving down the lakefront now. You could see the water, made choppy by wind, cold blue tipped with white. You could see buildings on the other side, tall glass facades, anonymous.

"Do you watch the game, Georgie?" asked Shannon.

He nodded. "Yeah. Yeah."

"Who's your favorite?"

He looked at her, at her perfect face, at her eyes, so like the eyes on his poster, now torn and thrown out with the trash. He answered softly.

"You are."

"Then why aren't you at home in your VR chair?"

He let his gaze drop to her hand, on his. How warm it felt, how soft. He had never thought about her hands before, not by themselves.

Hands, just hands.

"I had to come," he said.

"To see me?"

"Yeah."

"Why, Georgie? Don't you love the game?"

He didn't answer, not as he looked at her face again. It was stupid, but not. It was senseless and even now he was finding it hard to believe that she had done what she did, that somehow he had been different from all those other people, that she had taken him with her, that she was talking with him now. The words came then and with them he too understood.

"I was afraid for you."

The car turned into the museum parking lot.

The world knew at the speed of light. What is she doing? Who is he? Let's look at the vid again.

I don't know, Jeff. I don't like this at all.

The security man scanned him.

Still, she's got no right to do this. What if he's got something the man missed?

He's in the car with them.

That's not good enough. She's all we've got, you know. She represents America and she's got no right to go doing things like this.

I think it's related to the kidnapping. Someone messed with her head.

I think she's cracked because of Alicia.

She's got no right to be cracked.

I heard the police have an ID.

Who?

They won't say.

They ought to arrest the punk.

Wait! They're pulling into the museum. Watch!

Remember. The car stopping, the door popping open. Shannon first, and the crowd there crying out for her. A hush then, as Georgie followed, for they in all the world were away from their vids and had not heard. The security man then, joined by others, falling into a cordon around them, pressing them forward.

Look at the close-ups. Shannon has Georgie's hand in a tight grip and you can see the fear in his eyes.

But hers show something different.

Into the building now, away from the commercial vids. Security tapes now, showing it all.

A man, a game official in a suit and tie, standing there, blocking the way.

"Miss O'hea."

She nodded. The man did not move.

"Who is this, Miss O'hea?"

"This is Georgie Collins."

No motion. No sound, for the roar of the crowd outside is blocked by the heavy doors behind them.

"I'm afraid Mr. Collins will have to wait here," the official said. "We cannot allow him upstairs."

Shannon did not move. Georgie watched her, watched the man, eyes moving back and forth, back and forth. He bit at his lower lip.

"He is my friend," Shannon said. "I want him with me. I have a right."

"No." The official shook his head.

Above, Tanya and her Matron were looking down, watching. They could not see Shannon's eyes, how they were not the eyes on the posters and vids and commercials. There was no girl in them, no sweet innocence, no childish sparkle. Not at all, now, but cold, hard. A woman's eyes, certain and sure. The eyes of an adult, uncompromising. And when Shannon spoke her voice matched those eyes and it was not the Shannon we knew.

"I see. Very well, then. Please give Tanya my congratulations. Good day."

She turned before he could answer, managed to take two steps toward the door before one of the security men stepped in front of her.

And the official called out: "Miss O'hea!"

She turned. Her hand was still locked on Georgie's and he turned also.

"Miss O'hea, you can't!"

Her voice was low, deadly.

"I will."

Outside, we waited. Billions in their VR chairs. Commercials ready to run, endorsements ready to be heard. Anticipation waiting to be fulfilled.

At any cost. We had already shown that, hadn't we? We had our tickets and we were ready for the show. We had already been pulled along, tempted, told that this was to be the greatest match in history, that to miss it was insanity. Things were different; Shannon had us, suddenly, for without her there would be no game, no glory, no joy beyond joy. Our path was set and there was to be no escape now.

So is it any wonder that the official called out to her again? Did he dare do otherwise?

Could you have?

"Shannon, wait! Wait!"

Shannon paused again, looked back. The official spoke and his voice was not the same.

"All right. All right. He can stay."

Forward, up the stairs. The commercial vids came back on and we saw Shannon and Tanya shake hands, step to the doors of their interface chambers. Georgie was with Shannon and Tanya was accompanied by her Matron. The doors closed and the cameras stayed on for a moment.

Were you one of the many? Did you listen to the sportscasters and agree? Did you think vicious, prurient thoughts about the little chamber? And did a part of you wish it was you she had chosen, you who would sit with her as she played with her heart and soul for Alicia?

I don't understand, Jeff. You say she threatened to forfeit?

That's what I heard.

This is insane.

She'd better give us one hell of a performance to justify this.

Inside, Shannon guided Georgie to the seat reserved for Matrons and sat him down. She released his hand, watched him.

"Are you all right, Georgie?"

"Yeah." He swallowed, nodded. His face was drawn now, uncertain. He scratched nervously at his neck.

"Georgie?"

Again, "Yeah."

"You said you were afraid for me."

"Yeah."

"Are you still afraid for me, Georgie?"

He shrugged. "I don't know."

"You know, you were right. Thank you."

He looked closely at her. The woman's eyes had passed but the expression was still not what he remembered. Something more, something complete. As though in fact she knew what she wanted, what she needed. He watched as she slipped from her shiny blue warmups and hung them by the door, as she turned and faced him again.

"Listen to me, Georgie. I need you. I need you to do whatever I say, or I will be lost. Do you understand?"

He nodded. It had been true all along; she had said it, just now. True what he had thought, what he had felt. She was in danger, Shannon was, and she could see that he wanted to help. But there was fear, too, in Georgie. This was not all what he had thought, and he knew that nothing he could do would protect her from the men outside, the men with guns and scanners, the men who had stared at him with those cold eyes as they had entered the museum.

How, then? What, then?

Shannon was looking at him again, so beautiful, so perfect. And somehow she was much more now than she had ever been in the matrices, and Georgie realized that it was because she was real, right here. Not a poster and not a vid, but a person and therefore a truth, bound by the reality and honesty of the mundane.

A voice, finally, over the speakers.

"Kirilova, O'hea."

Shannon stepped to him, kissed him lightly on the forehead.

"Thank you, Georgie," she whispered, and then she was climbing into the VR chair as the lights dimmed.

Chapter 22

Final game. Last game. End game. You and me and billions more, waiting and watching in virtual reality. Mouths dry in anticipation, forgetting the shock of Alicia, the surprise of Shannon, forgetting what the sportscasters told us to remember from last year.

Tanya, descending, over there. Preparing, spinning once or twice, beautiful and radiant and honest and good.

Oh! Oh!

Shannon, appearing. Lovely, starlight in her hair. A wave, a passage of her unreal hand.

Ahh...

Watch now, prepare. This is it.

Symmetry, motion, drawing ground, anticipating. A probe, from Tanya, extending in impossibility. But Shannon was gone, and then back, and then gone again. Bytes in billions, constructs, unreal mathematics reflecting unreal beauty, bathing the billions in unreal love.

Watch as it builds.

For the real match was starting now. There is an ease that the brilliant have when they work their niche, a simplicity that is founded on instinct and practice, a sense that anyone can do the impossible just as they do. This was Tanya; this was Shannon. Constructing, disassembling, passing data and machine perfection through their ideal souls.

Ah! Look! Look!

Five minutes.

Tanya, with a new move, an impossible move. Shannon turned, dodged, countered. Tanya is up! She's pursuing!

Oh, God.

Shannon pulls back; look! Watch! A ripple, perfect, of love, comes, rises, falls.

Ten minutes.

Tanya answers with passion. I love! I love!

Time is shifting. You do not know time, in your VR chair. None of you. None of the billions knows of themselves, what they are, who they are. Shannon and Tanya are all there is, all that is real. They are in your brain, high, where thought and philosophy and knowledge reside, in that place where you are self-aware. True joy, absolute joy. You cannot defend against it.

Fifteen minutes.

More! More!

This is more!

Heart and lungs, muscle and bone, all work for this, for only this, for these girls whose perfection of being is in your mind, deep in there now. You know the matrices; you *are* the matrices.

Twenty minutes.

Tanya moving, anticipating. She is still playing the game, still trying to find that weakness that will bring Shannon down. But were you watching? Were you listening? Shannon is not playing anymore. No attack, no defense, but more.

Twenty-five minutes.

More. Deep inside you, all of you, all of the billions. Not high brain anymore, not middle brain, but low brain. She dances in the foundation of who and what you are, in that secret place no one should go.

Thirty minutes.

But she is there. It is not a match now, not a competition. Shannon battles Tanya, exchanges with her blow by blow. But she is not talking to Tanya, not seeing her. Tanya is only at one level, the one level that is the game. She is brilliant there, astounding and glorious, but Shannon is the whole network, everything. And because we are hooked in, we feel, you and I, just as she does.

Thirty-five minutes.

There are no words for it; there cannot be. Because words are reason, are logic and syntax and rules imposed. No. Shannon is showing us pure emotion, raw and honest. True and direct, unbounded by our presumptions and our prejudices and our society.

She is showing us how she feels.

Do you remember? Where were you?

Where were you when she showed us Alicia? Where were you when she played out before us the sight of her friend, lying in the hospital bed, walking as she was led, face blank and unseeing? Or when the anguish rose, running straight to your honest self?

This was my friend.

We did this to her.

Did you know fear, and sadness, then? Did you feel all that Shannon felt?

We did this.

You did this.

This is wrong.

Remember?

Tanya backed away. It was not fair to her, to have to be in the matrices like that, to have to see what happened to Alicia firsthand and then to face Shannon. She played still, with perfect, ideal love, but we could not see that love, for Shannon had taken the game to a new level and all we could know was her sadness and her anger. Shannon had cornered Tanya, wrapped her up in impossibilities, awaiting the final blow.

Go back. Remember that moment, when Shannon spoke and all the world heard.

Never again.

A moment, and we wept.

For we understood. Finally and honestly we knew. All that was Shannon, really Shannon. All her love, her real love, for her mother and her father and her brother, and for her friend. And more than that too. We knew her anger, her pain, her anguish and her uncertainty. All that was Shannon was us and with this came new knowledge.

What we were, too. How we had used them, the girls, how we had cared not for them but for their skill. Their love was a thing we wanted and they as people were nothing to us. And as we wept we did not see, did not notice, as Shannon rose, up and out, leaving behind constructs to hold Tanya for a moment, leaving an echo, a shadow of herself that we thought was her.

Rising up and out from the VR chair, to where Georgie sat, watching her.

Remember?

Tanya, at that moment, could have won. The constructs were brilliant, near perfect, but Tanya was the second best in all the world and they were no match for her. She could have smashed them down, claimed the matrices. The world championship she had sought all her life would have been hers.

And yet she did not. Instead she stayed in her place, did nothing. We do not know why.

Across the hall from her, in the quiet interface chamber, Shannon looked up at Georgie.

He whispered her name, for he had seen none of this, none at all, though perhaps he did not need to; perhaps he already knew.

Shannon stood, took his hand and guided him to her place, lay him back and settled his head against the sensors.

He did not resist.

Epilogue
▼
———————————   ———————————

Where were you when the system went down?

In your chair, perhaps, fighting the anguish? Or like a few, had you managed to pull away, managed to break the connection, and were you now gasping for breath and shuddering at what you had seen?

No matter. In the network Shannon had left us desolation. Intersect was more than it had ever been: Love still, for Alicia, but anger too, at us, at the game and what it had done. Despair at the thought of life alone. Anguish at the final move.

Tanya saw it first. She tried to flee but could not.

And all around the world we saw.

Georgie.

I know you, Shannon. I want to protect you, Shannon.

For you.

You.

You.

Remember then?

< DATA LOCK INPUT

< IMPROPER FEED COMMAND

< BASE SUBROUTINE CONTACTLOSS

< SYSTEM ERROR ERROR ER#OR!ROR!S*F@J#U$%&!#%^)...

The techs moved quickly to stop it but they were only human. At the speed of light that which was Georgie, which was male absolutely, raced around the world, into the game, into the matrices. Overload feeds began, built and grew, turning masses of silicon chips into slag, rerouting a hundred trillion commands through circuits designed for a billion.

Count now.
One thousand one.
One thousand two.
One thousand three.
One thousand four.
And it was over.
All over.

Security burst into Shannon's interface chamber with guns drawn, but Georgie was already up, protesting weakly that he was a boy and that she shouldn't make him do this, and Shannon was holding him close as he cried. They pulled them apart, handcuffed Georgie, hustled him outside. One guard stayed by Shannon, watching her. Outside, one of the vids was still on.

Watch this one.

Shannon emerges, the guard beside her. He is uncertain, for it will be a few seconds before the command comes down that Shannon O'hea is to be arrested, taken away, questioned. Watch her, though. See her face. Beautiful now, yes? But more, if you look. Just before they appear with the handcuffs, with the anger and the accusations, she smiles, just a bit, not like you've ever seen before.

It is a rare smile.

Because it is hers.

There was a trial, of course, and they played it on the vids. Great anger at first, indignity that Shannon and Georgie had robbed us of something so precious. For the system was down, completely; damage was worldwide and ran into the trillions of dollars.

Georgie first. Why? they asked. Why? He had no answer, only fear. Why? Why?

I don't know.

You ruin the world and you don't know?

No, please, I'm sorry...

You don't know?

Shannon did.

She told the world. It was not him at all, not his idea, not his plan. I brought him in. I sat him down. His only crime was loving me.

And that was no crime at all, remember?

We watched. He was such a little boy, sitting there, somehow too young for his suit and tie, but as we watched we began to see, and as we listened we began to hear.

No crime at all.

All right, we'll be lenient. Psych evaluation for him, some time in a JD home.

We turned to Shannon then, beneath the hot lights of the vid, sitting calmly beside her mother in the courtroom. Her eyes were cold, unforgiving. Who was trying who?

Shannon, we asked. Why?

Why?

Cold days. Harsh days. Our leniency towards Georgie had not sated our desire for revenge and we were prepared to pass stern judgment. Cold eyes as we spoke. The pleasure of the many outweighs the needs of the few. You have destroyed something that wasn't yours, Shannon. You have deprived the world of joy and every other girl of a chance to make it. What gave you that right?

She stood before us and answered slowly.

Were you watching the match, Judge?

Yes, of course.

And you, Madame Prosecutor? Were you listening?

Silence. The vid shows their faces; the Prosecutor looking down, into her briefcase, as though she wants to crawl in there and hide. The Judge stares straight ahead, twiddling his pen in one hand. The Prosecutor speaks then, one word. It is the same word that is on everybody's lips.

"Yes."

Then you already know.

There was prison, for a while. A special prison because she was a juvenile and more special still because she was a celebrity. But there seemed no point to it, really, as time went by, because most of us *had* been watching and we knew the truth, that we were as guilty as she was. We had made the game, had made her, and we had used her too, with excuses of payment and affection that we only intended to supply so long as she was convenient, so long as she served us. But now there was no game anymore, no Intersect, because the drive to rebuild the system had vanished even before Georgie brought it down.

And life went on, didn't it?

Is it really so bad?

It's late now. The fire has died down and I can feel the night in my bones. You seem thoughtful. Have you answered your question, appeased your hunger?

Not quite?

Very well. Listen.

If you drive south of Albuquerque, New Mexico, along the Interstate and the Rio Grande, you may pass without knowing it a large house surrounded by a high wall. Two women live there; one is a blonde and she is, in a strange and special way, beautiful.

The other woman has darker hair and a smile, and she is remarkably skilled with her hands, sculpting things in clay that are simple yet somehow complex, as though deep in her mind there is much more than you can see. She doesn't say much because speech is difficult for her, and at times she will begin to walk in a circle and will not be able to stop until the first woman guides her to a chair.

They do not go out much, these two women; you can see the blonde on occasion shopping for food in Los Lunas and once in a while the two of them will drive up to Albuquerque for something. Their neighbors know them and who they are, but they remember too and they understand.

Once in a while a man arrives on the magtrain from Denver. He rents a car and drives out to the house, where he stays for a few hours, perhaps a day. He is middle aged and his hair is thinning, and when he comes the same good neighbors see him and sometimes wave as he passes, for they know him too. He has a life and this is part of it, an aside he cannot quite forget. He does not know why he comes; nor do they; his wife and children know he is here but do not protest.

It is the first woman, always, who answers the door. The man will stand there, his hat in his hand, his face gentle and perhaps just a bit unbelieving, really, that he is here. The woman will smile at his gentle face and speak softly.

"Come in."

He does. If it is winter she takes his coat and hangs it in the closet by the door. They step into the garden, the two of them, and sit. Often the second woman is there, and if she is not she always joins them quickly. Her hands are usually covered with a thin layer of clay, and she picks at it as it dries against her skin.

"How are Charlotte and the boys?" the first woman will ask.

The man nods. "Fine…fine…" he says. "And Leonard? His family?"

"Good."

The conversation varies then; perhaps the woman will tell him that they saw a whooping crane at the Bosque, or he will tell how it snowed six inches in Denver last week and the mountains were beautiful. Eventually the first woman rises to fetch some tea and the man talks slowly with the second.

"You look well."

"Thank, you also."

She smiles, for him, and for the first woman, but for few others. It is a lovely smile and he knows what a gift it is. Often she will hold it until after the first woman returns, and on rare occasion she will still have it when she climbs into bed that evening. But more often it fades as they sit and drink their tea and chat, for always the conversation turns to the past, and in each of their eyes there is reflected a side to it that you and I cannot fully know.

I remember.

I too.

Yes.

Come, now. You expect more? But what more is there? It is a mundane conversation; three unremarkable, anonymous people. Yes, they were more, once. They stood before the world and we watched. And each of them was what we expected them to be.

Each of them wears that truth, always.

Look! An ember still burns in our fireplace. See the glow? It is what is left, now, of the raging flame that once warmed us, and that could burn us if we drew too close. You want to know what has become of this man, of these women? You want an end that neatly closes?

Then look to our ember, glowing softly, burning hot and quiet. The game, the real game, was like that, long before computers and the matrices and the net made love burn too bright. It was these three and any like them, together. Familiar and honest and real.

You know this now.

You are a witness.

THE END

0-595-30435-4

Printed in the United States
16118LVS00002B/330